BURNING FLOWERS

Leah Cutter

Knotted Road Press
www.KnottedRoadPress.com

Burning Flowers
Copyright © 2014 Leah Cutter
All rights reserved
Published 2014 by Knotted Road Press
www.KnottedRoadPress.com

Fox and Hound previous published in *Fiction River: Hex and the City,* edited by Kerrie Hughes
Sisters previous published in *Fiction River: Unnatural Worlds,* edited by Kristine Katheryne Rusch

ISBN: 978-1499260380

This book is licensed for your personal enjoyment only. All rights reserved. This is a work of fiction. All characters and events portrayed in this book are fictional, and any resemblance to real people or incidents is purely coincidental. This book, or parts thereof, may not be reproduced in any form without permission

BURNING FLOWERS

Leah Cutter

Also by Leah Cutter

Historic Fantasy:
Paper Mage
The Caves of Buda
The Jaguar and the Wolf

Contemporary Fantasy:
Clockwork Kingdom
Zydeco Queen and the Creole Fairy Courts
Siren's Call
The Popcorn Thief

Dark Epic Fantasy:
When the Moon Over Kualina Mountain Comes

The Shadow Wars Trilogy:
The Raven and the Dancing Tiger
The Guardian Hound
War Among the Crocodiles (summer 2014)

Collections:
The Shredded Veil Mysteries
Beyond the Garden
The Shadow Wars
Tell Me Again

Table of Contents

Fox and Hound	1
Old Friends	15
The Dutiful Daughter	29
Dragon's Son	43
The Tortoise and the Maiden	57
Sisters	67

Introduction

I've always been fascinated by China. I don't remember exactly where or when that fascination started. I do remember being only fourteen and begging to change schools so I could learn to speak Mandarin.

This collection contains a wide range of Chinese-inspired tales, from the contemporary urban setting of modern-day Bejing in *Fox and Hound*, to the historic pieces such as *Old Friends* and *Sisters*. It even contains science fiction, found in *Dragon's Son*.

I hope you enojoy this collection, that it inspires you to go do some more reading and studying of this fascinating land and culture on your own.

Leah Cutter
May 2014

Fox and Hound

"You need bicycle taxi? Rickshaw?" Gou asked for the tenthousandth time, smiling and trying to catch the eye of yet another tourist pouring off the late afternoon train from Hong Kong. He wore his second best shirt, the one with the fake American brand logo on the front pocket, that made him look more official, as well as his lightest-weight beige slacks, and rubber sandals. It was far too hot to wear jeans, though he had two pairs that he kept pristine and folded up at the noodle shop his mom ran.

Gou wasn't supposed to be in the West Beijing station, of course. The guards weren't supposed to let anyone without a ticket or a license into the huge concrete courtyard in the front of the massive station, let alone into the echoing, noisy halls close to the trains.

But Gou paid Shu (the fixer) well, and often, which got him into the station next to the staircase coming up from the trains, where he could get tourists to follow him before they headed to the subway stop. Stretching away from the bottom of the stairs and off into the distance were *li* upon *li* of railway lines going to places Gou had no hope of seeing. Loud speakers with polite, nasal accents announced the times and train numbers to places Gou had only heard about in stories told by his grandmother.

Only a few other bicycle taxi drivers were still waiting at the top of the stairs, mainly much older men who needed a fare as badly as Gou, but didn't speak enough English or wanted to work as hard. Gou's friends (and sometime competitors) were already gone: Hy with his official green uniform and colorful, laminated maps had snagged an entire group, while Long Yen with his charm and smile had persuaded an American couple to follow him.

"Best ride in town," Gou assured a western woman with strange blue eyes and brown curls poking around the sides of a wide brimmed hat. "Very smooth, very cheap." She shook her head and pulled the straps of her huge pack tighter, as if she was afraid Gou would rip it off her back.

Gou rolled his eyes and turned back to the few stragglers. He had to get a fare this afternoon. He needed the money. The platform in the back of his bicycle taxi, where his passengers put their feet, had broken off. He'd needed to buy a new one, and he'd had to pay to get it attached: The welder wouldn't barter trips with him.

Shu would be there tomorrow, demanding his cut. And Gou couldn't be short, or he'd lose his access to the train station. He might even be forced to join Hy, and work for a real company, where he'd never make enough money for his dreams. As an independent, if he hustled enough, at least he stood a chance.

Only a couple of straggling tourists remained, and they wouldn't even look at Gou, these tall white people with their big packs that they carried on both their front and back, as if they were taking all their possessions as well as their children with them.

The other drivers left, but Gou hung on, just for a bit, hoping.

Maybe he could work the northern night market tonight, hauling either drunken tourists or merchants and their goods. But the last time he'd done that, he'd ended up working for a fisherman and his cart had *stank* for a week.

However, he had to get the money somehow.

Gou turned to go and almost walked into an Asian man standing right beside him. "*Duibuqi*," he said, automatically apologizing.

The man replied in English. "You have a taxi?"

"Bicycle rickshaw," Gou said with his best customer smile. "Faster than cars and traffic," he assured the man.

His potential customer wore a crisp, white, short-sleeved shirt, brand new jeans, and Western sandals. He had a sharp nose and chin, like they'd been pinched out of clay. Freckles scattered across his nose, and his hair had been cut short, possibly too short, as it highlighted oversized ears and a broad forehead.

Beside the man, a large black trunk stood, almost waist high, with gold molding on the corners and around the lock.

"Best service in Beijing," Gou assured the man, reaching for the leather handle on the top of the trunk and tugging.

It didn't budge.

The man smiled at Gou. "Can you take me to *Huli Hutong*?"

"Of course," Gou boasted, though he had no idea where that was. If the man had actually pronounced the Mandarin correctly, it would have translated into Fox Lane. It didn't matter, though. Gou could find anything in this city.

The man laughed. "Very well, then," he said.

Just like that, the trunk came off the floor. It was heavy, and it didn't have wheels like most foreign luggage. However, Gou was young and strong, and he worked to make it look easy to carry. He led the way across the expansive, brown-marble entranceway, weaving around the huge pillars, and out into the soft night air.

The concrete courtyard was still full of people. Gou had heard more than one American tourist compare it to a football field. He glanced behind him, but his fare wasn't staring with wide-eyed amazement. He'd either been in China for a while, or he'd been here before.

Gou nodded to the boy who watched all the bikes, to make sure they didn't get stolen, past the other peddle cabs where the owners were stretched out, reading or napping, all the way to his own little brown and yellow cab.

His cab wasn't licensed, but Gou had spray painted numbers on the back of it, to make it look official. The brown seats were filled with rubber he'd scavenged from the side of the road, that his sister had sewn together. They smelled funny sometimes when it was too hot, but they were more comfortable than most of the other seats Gou had tried. The yellow cover that unfurled over the seats was patched, yet it was still mostly water proof. Gou kept the wheel bearings and the frame oiled and rust free, and the brakes tight.

"You from out of town?" Gou asked as he hoisted the trunk onto one side of the carriage.

"Yes, I'm visiting here from Japan," the man admitted.

Gou raised his eyebrows at that. China didn't have the greatest relationship with Japan, and Gou had met very few visitors from there. "Ah, *konichiwa*," Gou said, bowing his head.

The man replied with a flurry of Japanese.

Gou held up his hands and shook his head. "I only know a few words," he said. According to his mother, his father had been Japanese, or had come from there. But he hadn't stuck around, something Gou's step-father reminded him of at almost every dinner they ate together.

His mother had insisted that Gou learn a few words in the language, however, Gou hadn't stuck to it.

"Pity," the man said, peering closely at Gou. "I would have thought—never mind. You speak good English, though," he said, settling into his seat.

"Thank you," Gou said, climbing onto his bike. "I practice. But I need more." More work. More money. More time. More powerful relations who could smooth his way.

The man laughed. "We all need more," he said softly.

※ ※ ※

Gou bumped his way across the cracked concrete, up across the sidewalk, and into the bike lane along Fuxing Lu. He automatically started peddling east, going toward the heart of Beijing. It was late enough in the day that many workers rode around him on their black, sturdy bikes. Every time one passed Gou, they rang their bell. Cars filled the road, bumper-to-bumper. Pollution hazed the air across the eight lanes of traffic, and stank of rotten eggs, wood smoke, and burnt oil. Gou had worn his mask when he peddled into the station, but he couldn't put it on now: He didn't want to scare the tourist, and maybe not get a good tip.

"First time in Beijing?" Gou called out over his shoulder.

"No, no. I have family here," the man assured him.

When Gou stopped at Wanfeng Lu, he realized he didn't know where he was going. "*Huli Hutong*?" he called back as he stood on his peddles to get his bicycle moving again.

"Yes," the man replied.

Gou didn't have to look back to know he was being laughed at.

"It's near *Dai Tong*," the man called out helpfully.

Gou peddled and thought, rolling out a map of Beijing in his mind. *Dai Tong* neighborhood was south of the city, and not too far from the railroad station, just the next big circle in. It wasn't a tourist place, so he hadn't gone there often. But maybe…

"Is it near *Ji lu*?" Gou asked, remembering a small neighborhood near the east corner of *Dai Tong*—Chicken Street, close to a night market that specialized in many chicken dishes, from feet to butts to tongues.

Plus, wouldn't the foxes want be close to the chickens?

"Very good!" the man called out.

Pleased, Gou peddled faster. Though he didn't know exactly where he was going, at least he wouldn't be circling forever. Maybe he could get a fare from the market there, before heading back home to the noodle house.

The light dimmed and night settled in as Gou turned off the main thoroughfare and onto the side streets. Few cars remained here, and they were happy to blast their horns at him, making him jump, or blinding him with their lights. But it was only a few more blocks before he could slip into the smaller hutong streets, where cars weren't allowed.

Gou didn't mind driving down a hutong during the day, but he hated it at night: Light came only from a few lanterns hanging outside of house gates, as well as from windows. No overhead lights lit the narrow alleyways. It was impossible to avoid the deep ruts in the road, or the broken stones. He winced every time he heard the board in the passenger cab groan. He didn't have the money to fix it again.

The smell of chicken and garlic, frying in a wok, floated out to Gou. He hadn't eaten dinner—and he was never sure if his mom would leave anything for him at the noodle house. He couldn't afford much, not even with this fare, not with Shu's bribe due.

Beyond the tall walls that lined the tiny street, Gou heard the occasional radio or TV. They passed a doorway where half a dozen old men sat out on small chairs on the stoop, drinking shots. Two girls in navy blue, school uniforms walked slowly down the lane, only stepping to the side when Gou rang his bell.

"Turn here!" the man suddenly called out.

Gou turned immediately. An open gate sprang up before him, with a peaked roof and plain walls. He barely missed the edges, but managed to drive his cab directly through the center.

Hushed air fell on Gou, making him slow down. The street here was even more narrow, and the old stone houses were only a few feet apart. Trees grew next to the walls, shading the street. Broken flagstones marred the path.

"Then another right here," the man said, his quiet voice echoing in the small space.

Gou pulled out of the tight alley into a broader street. It was funny—he couldn't hear the traffic beyond the walls, not even the motorcycles. And the air smelled sweeter. It didn't burn his lungs like the badly polluted air of Beijing usually did.

There were no cars to be seen, not even parked, even though it was wide enough to hold them. Tall, brick fences lined the street, with doors that still glowed brilliant red even in the dark. Old fashioned lanterns hung outside each. Large, graceful trees rose up to form an arch overhead. Sweet night jasmine bloomed in the gardens. Gou's tired legs suddenly felt refreshed, as though he could peddle for ten thousand *li*.

"Down at the end of the street," the man said.

Gou nodded as he pulled into the cul-de-sac. The gate at the end was larger than the ones he'd passed. It must lead to a *shiheyuan*, or traditional courtyard. He could only imagine what lay beyond the gate, the many buildings lining the center square, the garden of brilliant flowers that he could almost smell, the burbling fountain that would give him peace in the middle of the night.

Gou pulled himself out of his day dream and turned to say, "Here?"

But the man had already hopped off Gou's bike and was tugging the large trunk to the ground.

"Let me help," Gou said, about to slide off his bicycle.

"No, no. Stay there," the man insisted. "You must not get off your bike."

"Really?" Gou asked.

The man gave him a toothy smile, like a foreigner. "Trust me. You need to stay on it."

Gou thought it was strange, but he did as he was told.

"How much do I owe you?" the man asked, getting out his wallet.

Gou quoted four times his usual price, expecting him to bargain.

The man didn't even blink. He just counted out the *yuan* from a thick wad.

Gou could have kicked himself. He should have asked for more. The man could obviously afford it.

At least now he'd be able to pay Shu.

"Go straight back out the way we came in," the man instructed. "And don't get off your bike. You shouldn't have any trouble."

"Thank you," Gou said, carefully folding the bills, then shoved them into his front pocket. "*Xie xie nin.*"

"You're welcome," the man replied, waving him off and turning toward the gate.

Gou waited, hoping to catch a glimpse of what was inside the gate, but the man slipped through more quickly than Gou would have imagined, especially given that large trunk.

He sighed, then shook his head. Nothing more to do here but head back. He didn't need to get another fare, but maybe he could stop by the night market anyway, just in case his luck was still running hot.

Then Gou's stomach rumbled, reminding him that he hadn't eaten dinner yet.

Gou rode alone the open street, still marveling at how quiet and peaceful it all seemed. He nearly missed the alley, but luckily he was going slowly enough that he could bump into it.

Strange, though. Where had that temple come from? He hadn't seen it on the way in. He would have remembered the great rock *steeles* rising in front of it. Maybe he should stop and read what was carved into their sides—then his stomach rumbled again, and he passed by.

Then the gate he'd first come through rose in front of him. Good. He was going the right way.

Suddenly, from beside the gate, a great dog sprang out of nowhere. It looked like a Doberman, with great teeth and glowing red eyes. It leaped straight for Gou.

Gou kicked out with his foot, giving the dog a good hit in the face. The dog lunged again, but Gou kept going, peddling with one foot while kicking with the other.

He had to get out of there.

The dog charged one last time, banging into the back of Gou's rickshaw. He heard the metal groan, but he righted himself and peddled madly, popping through the gate.

Noise and light and the sour stench of pollution all returned suddenly. Gou stood on the brakes to slow down, then looked over his shoulder.

No dog from his nightmares bounded up after him.

And no gate stood behind him. It was just a blank wall. As if it had never been there.

Gou dismounted his bike, his legs shaking. If he'd fallen off, touched the ground in that cursed hutong, he would have been stuck there forever. He just knew it. It was like one of those fairy tales his grandmother had told him, though she'd always said the fox fairies were good.

But he'd escaped! Gou pumped his fist. What a story he had to tell his friends, later.

Then Gou stuck his hand in his pocket.

Instead of a nice folded square of *yuan*, he pulled out a crumpled pile of dead leaves.

Gou may have escaped, but he'd been cheated out of his money.

※ ※ ※

As soon as Gou finished working in his mom's noodle shop the next morning, he peddled as fast as he could to *Dai Tong*, hunting for the man who had cheated him. The day had dawned hot and smoggy, the radio announcing yet again a smog index of one hundred eighteen, unhealthy for those sensitive to it. Gou wore his mask wrapped tightly across his face, as well as the same clothes he'd worn the day before.

The wall where the gate had been was still blank, made out of plain, gray brick. On the other side of the wall stood a house. Now, in the light of day, Gou could tell that this hutong wasn't one of those that had tours or tourists: The nearby walls slumped and were broken along the edges, the clay tiles on roofs were shattered, and laundry hung between the houses, like colorful flags. This was a place where people lived, not a park with tours. He could hear children playing just a few doors down, and the smells of thick *jitang* and spicy ginger floated to him.

The man was nowhere to be seen. Gou peddled through all the back lanes of *Dai Tong* before he raced to the train station, hoping to pick up at least one fare before Shu arrived and demanded his bribe.

The gods seemed to smile on Gou that morning, and he got double his normal fare from a Norwegian tourist with bad breath who was looking for, "Beer, beer, and more beer!" Gou was even able to pay Shu, counting out the *yuan* into his fat, sweating palm. Gou wouldn't have enough for a single repair, not even a flat tire, but the next fare should fix that.

Or finding the man who'd cheated him.

Every day, Gou spent his extra hours seeking the man, peddling through back alleys and tiny, twisted streets that no devil could follow. He even talked with some of the older peddle cab drivers, seeing if they had ever gone to either *Dai Tong* or heard of *Huli Hutong*, but none of them had.

It was early evening almost a month later when Gou finally found his prey. He was navigating *Yingtao San Hutong*, a very thin alley: If he'd had two passengers, each would have been able to touch a gray brick wall. The smog had thinned, and though the air index was above fifty, Gou wasn't wearing his mask. In the alcove next to him, neighbors had hung half a dozen birdcages, each holding a bright green or yellow songbird that sounded clear notes through the night.

Despite the cramped lane, a broom merchant had put out a big box out in front of his shop, with different types of brooms sticking out of it: Modern brooms made from bright blue and red plastic, western style brooms made of yellow straw, as well as traditional wooden brooms with brown branches tied to the end.

Gou slowed down even further, standing on the peddles while he waited for two high school girls in their uniforms to pass by first, admiring their white shirts and green plaid skirts. When he looked back up, he spied the man he was seeking coming out of the shop.

Without thinking, Gou slammed down on his peddles, flying forward and nearly running into the man.

The shop keeper came out from his doorway yelling, but Gou ignored him, focusing on the man carrying an odd shaped broom. "You cheated me," he said, getting off his bike.

"And you found me. Astonishing. You've been looking for a while, haven't you?" the man responded in perfect Mandarin.

"I have," Gou said, pulling up. The man had never spoken Mandarin before. He was Japanese, right?

"It's alright," the man said, both to the shopkeeper and to Gou. "This is my ride."

"Only if you pay me first. With real money," Gou said hotly. He wasn't about to be fooled again.

The man considered him. "Can you find your way to *Huli Hutong* by yourself?"

Gou bit his lip. He wanted to say that of course he could. But he hadn't been able to find it, not after all his weeks of hunting.

"I will pay you double if you can get into the hutong alone," the man said, settling into the passenger cab of Gou's bike.

Gou refused to climb back onto his bike. "You pay me what you owe me. Now. In real money."

The man took out his wallet and carefully counted out the bills, like he had the first time. He waved them toward Gou, then took them back. "I could pay you this, now. And that would guarantee that you'd never see me again. No matter how hard you look. Ever. Or," the man continued slyly. "You could listen to a proposal."

"You haven't said anything of interest, yet," Gou said, scowling.

"I'm impressed that you found me, actually. You have potential, and I have a possible business deal," the man said calmly. "I want you, exclusively, to carry me and my family. You will need more bikes, motorbikes, even, and I will pay for them. You will own a whole fleet of cabs that cater to us. But you have to be able to get to my home on your own. You've already proved that you can get out."

"You set that dog on me?" Gou asked hotly. He still had nightmares about those red eyes, though he told himself that it must have been a trick of the light.

The man shrugged. "You passed that test." He leaned forward. "Now pass this one." For a moment his eyes held a soft purple glow, then they faded back to plain black.

How could Gou find the unfindable? The street wasn't on any map, the hutong not in any history of the neighborhoods.

Still, Gou had to try, though Hy and Long Yen and everyone would call him a fool for not taking the money in hand and running.

With a sigh, he got back onto his bike, standing on the peddles to get the vehicle moving.

The man laughed in the clear evening air. "You have until midnight," he declared as he climbed onto his seat. "The hunt is on!"

Gou wasn't certain, though, if he was the fox or the hound.

※ ※ ※

It had grown dark by the time Gou reached *Dai Tong*, however, he was very familiar with the neighborhood now. He peddled directly to the place where he'd first seen the gate to *Huli Hutong*, though it was just a wall, as always. He rode next to the wall slowly, constantly looking up from where he was going to the plain brick, hoping to catch a glimpse of an opening, but he never saw one.

They passed dark doorways, closed shops, and barred windows, all the life tucked away behind the steep walls. Gou felt like the fences were closing in on him, the small alley growing more narrow. He didn't have a watch, or really, anything to tell time with: It was no longer ancient times, with bell towers ringing the double hours. Still, he knew it was late, and growing later.

Gou peddled faster, popping out of the lane and into a wider street. The cars there honked at him, flashing their lights, but he didn't care. He pulled in front of them, racing, his legs pumping, as he turned sharply, going back into the neighborhood, taking them down an even smaller alley.

If Gou leaned to the side, he could run his fingers along the wall here. He neatly avoided the flower box on his right, the sour smell of geraniums floating up to him, then the raft of bicycles all chained to a long metal pipe on his left. He still didn't see an entrance, though he slowed down and kept swiveling his head, looking from side to side.

They went down another alley, then another, always circling back to *Dai Tong*.

Finally, the man said, "Not everything can be seen."

Gou wanted to shout at his passenger. He knew that. He'd been looking and looking, and he'd never been able to find the entrance, find his way back into that quiet street.

As they reached the end of the alley, Gou paused. *Huli Hutong* hadn't just been beautiful to look at, it had also smelled wonderful, like sweet lilies. It had felt different too, the air softer, more humid. There hadn't been any traffic noises; it had been quiet. He was sure there were fountains that sang cheerfully behind the courtyard walls, and that the rice there would be fragrant and delicious.

Maybe Gou couldn't find it with his eyes. But with his ears, and his nose, and his mouth...

Gou erupted out into the wider street, urging his tired legs to go faster. He'd traveled far that day, but he was determined to go further yet. The car behind him honked angrily and swerved. Gou waved at him in apology, racing down the wide street, taking them back to the first alley, where he'd seen the gate.

Then Gou slowed down. He knew this alley, had boasted to his friends about how well he knew it now, since he'd been down it so often, searching. So he closed his eyes, coasting, no longer peddling, and lifted his nose high.

There, to his right, jasmine beckoned. He turned his head toward it, pressing his cheek against the softer air. It was quieter there as well.

When Gou opened his eyes, he still didn't see anything but a blank wall. The hutong was there, though. The opening. Right beyond the wall.

Gou stood up on his peddles to stop his bike, then started peddling backwards, backing up his cab.

He needed speed if he was going to do this right.

And if he crashed into the wall, well, that was the will of the gods.

"Hold on!" Gou called to his passenger. He closed his eyes again and slammed down as hard as he could on his peddles. The cab leaped forward, as if it were a living animal and not made of steel and rubber.

Gou kept his nose high, seeking the start of that scent. When the air grew sweeter, and it suddenly grew quiet, he turned abruptly and opened his eyes.

The peaked gate loomed ahead of him. Gou skidded through the turn and passed through the opening with barely an inch on his right side.

"Well done," his passenger said.

Gou breathed deeply, feeling the peace settle into his bones. He was finally here. At last.

※ ※ ※

Gou waited in the train station, this time right outside the exit of the customs hall. He wore a better shirt now, white with a tiny red fox embroidered over the left pocket, as well as finely made black pants, and soft leather sandals. He carried a small whiteboard with the name of his client written on it, in Japanese kanji, Chinese characters, and English.

Just like all the other official licensed couriers.

It wasn't difficult to spot his client through the sea of travelers pouring out of the door: She was cute, with freckles scattered across the bridge of her nose, and a stillness that ebbed out of her, quieting everyone who stayed for a while in her presence. She wore her long black hair back, hiding her overly large ears, with bangs over her broad forehead. She wore a simple white-and-purple striped blouse over a straight black skirt.

"*Liequan*," she said, smiling, coming up to him.

"*Huli*," he replied. It was part of the code of the family, as well as a greeting: Hound and fox.

Gou collected her bags, carrying them easily despite their weight, like all the other official couriers did. He politely asked about her trip, but that was all, her stillness affecting him too.

Instead of leading her out to the rows of limousines and state cars, though, Gou walked her across the broad concrete courtyard in the front of the station to the rows of peddle cabs. Gou's company colors were brown and yellow, with real licenses and enough bribes that he could reserve the front parking spots.

The young woman clapped her hands with delight when she saw Gou's peddle cab. "Papa arranged for you," she said, settling into the back of Gou's cab.

"Of course," Gou replied. He'd learned a lot about his clients since that first trip on his own to *Huli Hutong*: They didn't like automobiles, and merely tolerated motorbikes when they needed speed. They preferred old-fashioned things, like handmade brooms and rickshaws.

Once all her luggage was strapped in, Gou started off at a leisurely pace, letting his client enjoy the city. Cars along the wide road raced past them, as did students on their bicycles, their bells ringing merrily. Gou took his time, though. He no longer had to hustle, racing for just one more fare.

Gou actually no longer needed to peddle a cab himself, he could have hired one more rider, but he liked to pick up family members himself: It kept his patron happy, helped smooth out any bumps in their relationship. Plus, he'd met other, stranger beings this way, building his network, hoping to become the exclusive carrier to all the spirit creatures and their kind.

Later that afternoon, Gou would take the daughter on a tour, through the tourist *hutongs*, as well as the secret, hidden ones that only the fox fairies could find.

And a few, well-trained hounds.

Old Friends

"Are you all being willfully stupid? Or merely idiots?" Wei Fu thundered at his students. His words echoed through the plain classroom, bouncing through the open windows at the far end and out into the wide courtyard. But he was no *Lei Gong*: His mere ire didn't rattle the beautiful painted scrolls of calligraphy on the walls.

Of course, his students all sat too far away for him to see their expressions clearly. No matter how Wei Fu squinted, the world was always fuzzy. But he could imagine the usual shock and dismay clearly, marring their perfectly schooled expressions above their clean, white student robes.

When no one dared say anything, the dozen of them kneeling and crouched around their low wooden desks, fiddling with brushes and scrolls and looking anywhere but him, Wei Fu said, "Fine. For tomorrow read *Táng lù* articles four, five, and eight in section one, and be prepared to recite the articles on transfer of land from an unlucky widow with no children." He turned away, gathering up the scrolls he'd used for class that day. At least they were all copies from his own hand, written out with large enough characters that he could easily read them.

"Which articles, Master Wei?" Deng Wu asked.

Even with his faulty vision, Wei Fu recognized the smarmy smile. Deng Wu thought he was clever and charming, and that his family name and influence could win him the civic exams and a cushy position in the government.

"If you can't name the articles on the transfer of land, do you really belong in this class with these other esteemed students?" Wei Fu asked, using his kindest voice, the one he would actually use with an unlucky widow wanting to transfer her land.

He continued to roll up his scrolls, as if all his attention was on them and not the troublesome students in front of him, the ones who had thought it funny to move the front table, so Wei Fu had walked into it. They'd only done that once, though. Such disrespect had earned them a stern lecture from Chao Xi, Wei Fu's old friend and head administrator for the school.

Deng Wu's scowl almost made Wei Fu smile. But he maintained his stern *laoshur* demeanor.

"Tomorrow," Wei Fu told them again.

When he bowed to his students, they rapidly rose and bowed much lower in return, showing the proper respect. At least that much had been beat into them.

If only they would show the law the same care. It was what separated all of them from the barbarians, what gave the Middle Kingdom structure and civility that foreigners could only dream of.

Wei Fu swept from the classroom. He only had a little time, but it was enough. He could go to the soup stand near the market, the one he liked and always ate at, before making his way back to the law office. He stepped out of the darkened school corridor and into the sunny courtyard. Dirt paths cut across the wide yard, while cedar trees crowded up against them, giving the air a sweet scent. Other students hurried by, bowing their heads quickly as Wei Fu passed, showing proper if too rapid respect.

The school compound took up most of the block. By cutting through the courtyard, Wei Fu could save even more time. Which meant he might get an extra contract copied this afternoon, which meant he could save more *bao* coin. Maybe he could persuade his old friend Chao Xi, the head administrator, to give him another class this winter. Old Jing would give him more mornings away from the law office. Then he could—

"Master Wei. Master Wei!"

Wei Fu stopped at the eager young voice. He turned, blinking in the bright summer sunlight.

From under the huge cedar trees came one of the shorter, fatter students, wearing plain dark-blue robes.

Wei Fu returned the student's bow, puzzling over who had stopped him. He didn't remember this young man from his classes, with a barrel chest and almost no neck.

"So glad to meet ya, Master Wei. I'm Fat Ang."

Wei Fu peered more closely at the student. He'd only taught a few classes at the school, and though he hadn't bothered to learn all of his student's names, Fat Ang still didn't look familiar.

"I ain't had the privilege of bein' in your class," Fat Ang said helpfully.

Wei Fu examined Fat Ang's robes—they seemed reasonably made, and his sandals were typically worn by students, though his accent placed him firmly in the fields.

Was this Fat Ang even a student? His robes weren't white. However, he was wearing a student badge on his left shoulder, eight sided and embroidered with yellow and blue—something. Some design that Wei Fu had never bothered to bring close enough to his poor eyes to see.

"I attended that lecture you did last month," Fat Ang continued. "On using the land code section of the *Táng lù* to clarify the penal code sections. It was great."

"I see," Wei Fu said, mollified.

Hadn't his own dear mother told him that he shouldn't judge a man's kindness by his robes, just his wealth? And wasn't that the point of the civic exams? To get the brightest and most talented men into the civil service, not merely the wealthiest either in coin or *guanxie*, favors extending for generations?

"How can I help you?" Wei Fu said, trying to keep the impatience out of his voice.

Old Jing would just have to understand if Wei Fu was tardy. Educating the next generation was important work.

"Please, Master Wei, you were on your way some wheres?"

"Lunch," Wei Fu admitted.

"Can I walk with you? I'll pay," Fat Ang said.

"Of course," Wei Fu said graciously, not saying anything about how the crass this young man's offer of money was. Really, he should just slip the vendor a few coins, on the side, not make any fuss about it or announce it. He obviously needed someone to show him the finer etiquette in these things.

They stepped out of the studious, quiet, school compound and into the busy street. The gate tower sounded the mid-day hour of the Horse. Laborers in their stained robes, merchants wearing fine, rich colors, and slaves in their loin cloths hurried on their business. Many food shops lined the dirt street and students lined up in front of them. Sweet corn soup, fatty meat, and spicy rice cakes all tempted Wei Fu, but he had his routine. He took long strides, jostling people from side to side, already regretting his soft heart. He had work to do!

However, Fat Ang seemed genuinely interested in the penal code and asked intelligent questions about offenses committed against persons and property, as well as offenses committed in the course of brawls.

After they finished eating at the small soup stand, Wei Fu bid Fat Ang a fond farewell. Though he'd done most of the talking, falling easily into lecture mode, Fat Ang had at least acted interested the entire time. Plus, he'd insisted they have *mung gao*, a small, sticky dessert that Wei Fu secretly adored.

Maybe this teaching thing had something to it, beyond earing a few more coins.

Wei Fu rushed across the market square toward the offices of Jing and Sons. He'd never thought about mentoring someone before, someone who might appreciate the finer nuances of the law. Wei Fu had never wanted to work in the governor's office, defending or examining criminals. He much preferred the more staid side, contracts and deeds, following the twisted paths of inheritance, using the trivia of ancient codes in the application of law.

As he hurried into the backdoor of the office, where he and the other clerks worked, he rolled up his sleeves, prepared to work long into the night so he could earn enough and finally fulfill his dearest dream: to start his own office.

❈ ❈ ❈

"Master Wei. Master Wei!"

Wei Fu stopped and waited impatiently for Fat Ang in the school courtyard. Leaves barely budded on the branches of the cedar trees, and spring rains had turned the usual dirt paths into muck.

"I'm sorry I don't have time today for lunch," Wei Fu said. His dear mother had been sick the previous evening and he needed to rush home to see her before going back to the offices.

Of course, he didn't mention that to Fat Ang, or to anyone. "Wear your broken arm *inside* your sleeve," that was what she'd said time and again. Fat Ang was a student, possibly a friend, but not an old friend.

"I understand," Fat Ang said, bowing.

Wei Fu bowed in return and started walking away.

"Ya gotta come to Sing's, later, though, to celebrate."

Wei Fu stopped and turned back. "Celebrate?" he asked, cocking his head to one side. The exam results hadn't been posted yet, had they?

"I have a premonition, you know. Of good things. Good fortune," Fat Ang said with a conspiratorial wink.

"I see," Wei Fu said, keeping his face pleasantly smooth. "Perhaps after dinner tonight."

Fat Ang rocked back on his heels. "Might be better if you came earlier," he said seriously. Then he gave a grin. "Sing's serves the best apple wine in Da Shan."

"If I can," Wei Fu told him, with one last nod. He hurried off, then paused in the doorway to the street.

The results hadn't been recorded, as far as Wei Fu knew. No one should be celebrating yet. He stood with one foot in the street, the other in the courtyard. He had things to do. He needed to go see his mother.

He still paused. Something about Fat Ang unsettled him: If he was honest, had been unsettling him for a while. Not his crass behavior or his accent—a scholar overlooked those sorts of things and saw through to the true mettle of a man.

But the sly digs Fat Ang had taken at Wei Fu's unmarried status, the questions he'd asked about brawling, and how he'd cross-examined Wei Fu, not about the exams, but about the process of judging it, who read the essays and when, all had Wei Fu questioning now.

With reluctance, Wei Fu turned back toward the school courtyard. Fat Ang was talking with another student under the cedar trees. Wei Fu squinted and took a step closer, then stepped to the side, off the path, and under the trees himself, carefully stepping over the wide puddle.

Fat Ang knew Deng Wu? That lazy, smarmy student of his? What were the pair of them conspiring to do?

As they walked off, Wei Fu hurried after them, thanking his mother and his ancestors for his long legs that let him easily keep up.

Inside the school, Wei Fu paused again, blinking rapidly to clear his eyesight. The corridor was so dark after the sunny courtyard, even with its whitewashed walls. Though many people filled the space, he still spotted his quarry, at the end of the hall, to the right. He hurried down the smooth brick floor, keeping to the side and behind other people when he could: not everyone had such bad eyesight as himself, and he was taller than most of the students and teachers, a dignified, easily recognizable target.

He needn't have bothered, though: the two students were intent on their task, heads together, scurrying toward the office of the secretary.

The man who recorded all scores.

Such a small link in the chain. Wei Fu marveled at the simplicity of it.

Wei Fu read the essays his students turned in, then either passed or failed each. He handed the list of names to the secretary, who recorded all scores for all students for the entire school.

Wei Fu never went back and verified that the list was accurately recorded, that at the end of the year, full marks were awarded to the proper students. He did recall how, the previous year, he'd been surprised that one of his students, who hadn't done well in his class, had managed to pass the final exams. He'd been magnanimous, though, assuming that it was merely his class that had tripped the boy up.

The secretary, a thin, pinched man whose name Wei Fu couldn't remember, came out and greeted the other two, bobbing his head rapidly, like an peach in water. Even Wei Fu could see his robes were in poor repair, and his sandals needed mending.

No cash exchanged hands. And the man obviously didn't like what he was being asked to do. He stormed back into his office with a huff and the two students bowed to each other. Deng Wu continued down the corridor, while Fat Ang headed back toward Wei Fu.

Heart thudding in his chest, Wei Fu looked for a place to hide in the wide corridor. There were no bookcases or convenient altars to duck behind. He was too tall, too well-known, for Fat Ang to miss. Wei Fu took a step backwards, directly onto the foot of his old friend, Chao Xi.

"Oh, I'm sorry," Wei Fu said, bowing low. "Please forgive my clumsiness."

Chao Xi laughed. "No, no, it was my fault, please forgive me."

"No, I insist, it was my fault," Wei Fu said, still bowing, glancing out of the corner of his eye, maintaining his low position until he was certain the student had passed. Only then did he straighten up.

"Why aren't you at your law office, scribbling away madly?" Chao Xi teased. "Don't tell me that you're actually taking a double-hour to yourself. That would portent the end of the empire!" Chao Xi face was engulfed in kindness, while his eyes were the sharpest of any Wei Fu had ever seen. He wore a dark blue robe, cut like a student's, but finely made and woven from silk and flax.

Wei Fu's heart warmed at his friend's jibes. "*Hrmph*," he said gruffly, though he knew he smiled as well. "You wouldn't know hard work if it wrapped you in a cloak and kidnapped you."

"Well, you wouldn't know an hour of ease if it did the same," Chao Xi pointed out.

Wei Fu *hrmphed* again, then grew serious. He looked up and down the hallway: Too many students and other instructors were still there. He knew this needed to be handled privately, but it also needed immediate attention.

"Come," Wei Fu said, tugging on the sleeve of his friend, dragging him into an empty classroom. The tables were aligned in straight rows, all the scrolls and folding books neatly put away. The order and quiet gave Wei Fu some much needed solace. He turned to his friend and asked, as kindly as he could, "What do you know of—what's his name—your secretary. The secretary for the school."

Chao Xi put his arms across his chest and tilted his head up. "What have *you* discovered?"

"You have suspicions, then?" Wei Fu tried to contain his excitement. It was still just an exercise, nothing conclusive.

Chao Xi bit his lips together for a moment, rocking back and forth, before he finally said, "There's been talk. Of students grades not recorded faithfully. A mistake or two, I can accept that. The school has been growing. More students, more grades, and still only one secretary."

"What about the civic exams?" Wei Fu asked, trying to stay nonchalant and failing.

Chao Xi stared with hard eyes at Wei Fu. "What have you heard?"

"I saw two students talking with the secretary. *After* one had invited me to a celebration. Because he had a 'premonition' of good news." Wei Fu paced between the low desks.

"Someone invited *you* to a celebration?"

"I do occasionally go out with friends," Wei Fu said hotly.

"You made friends with a student?"

"They aren't all idiots and imbeciles," Wei Fu protested. "He approached me first. And he asked intelligent questions. Then he listened to me talk. For hours and—"

"He didn't fall asleep once?" Chao Xi asked, interrupting.

"No, he asked me about..." Wei Fu stopped. "He was using me, wasn't he? To get information about the exam."

Chao Xi shrugged. "I don't know. Possibly." He regarded his friend with sad eyes.

"I've been a fool, haven't I?" The realization that he'd been used wrapped tightly around Wei Fu's heart and settled like a stone in his belly.

"You may have been, old friend," Chao Xi said. He came over to where Wei Fu had stopped and put a kind hand on his shoulder. "But we can make it right."

"We have no influence with this secretary," Wei Fu pointed out. Bile settled in the back of his throat. "And Deng Wu's too highly placed. We can't touch him."

Chao Xi pursed his lips, thinking. "Deng Wu may be. But Fat Ang isn't. You know the only reason he's in the school is because he blackmailed half the admissions council, right?"

"I didn't know," Wei Fu said, looking at the ground. Even with his poor eyesight he could tell his robes were stained near the bottom. Just like his life. A fitting end, really, since he was about to be dragged down into the muck if he challenged an important family. Or a snake like Fat Ang.

"You have to be kept out of this," Chao Xi said, as if he'd been reading his friend's thoughts.

"I am nothing," Wei Fu said. "My family name means nothing. You, on the other hand, have a successful career. I'm still scrabbling to get my own office. You also have a growing family. What, three boys now, and a fourth on the way?"

"If Bái Huā Bàn is generous," Chao Xi said.

"She will be, old friend," Wei Fu said.

He looked at Chao Xi, tall and thin, with rabbit-soft brown eyes and an easy smile, who made friends with everyone, from the poorest slave to the richest lords, who had so little guile in him it was as if he'd been born without a spleen.

Whereas Wei Fu had absorbed all the subtlety and nuance of the law.

"I will make this right," Wei Fu told Chao Xi. "I swear it. You cannot be involved. I was the fool."

"But—"

"I never talked with you today," Wei Fu instructed. "I left the classroom early because of my mother."

"Your mother?" Chao Xi asked sharply.

"Never mind. I must go now. It will all be settled tonight," Wei Fu said. "I promise."

And he intended to keep that promise, even if it meant hard labor for contributing to a brawl.

※ ※ ※

Wei Fu paid more of his hard-earned *bao* coin than he wanted to, but he got one of his nephews to run some errands for him, then to look after his dear mother, while at the same time, swearing not to saw a word about it to anyone, particularly not Wei Fu's older brother.

Full night had descended on Da Shan before Wei Fu finally staggered out into the street. Only a few people still scurried by. Lamps in the front windows and at the doorways of family compound were barely enough to cut through the deep shadows. The coolness refreshed him, and he was glad it had stopped raining.

Waving his wine pot, Wei Fu stumbled, dribbling a bit more on his robes. He'd taken a few mouthfuls of the stinging liquor, then spit them out, the back of his throat burning, his eyes watering. But he needed to reek.

Sing's was near the southern gate. Even the darkness couldn't hide the sagging roofs of the nearby buildings, the rubbish thrown into the street, the stink of the tannery. Wei Fu heard the boisterous group a block away, shouting obscenities and laughing crudely.

He almost took another swig of the bottle to fortify himself, if he'd thought such a thing would work.

"Fat Ang!" Wei Fu called as he climbed the steps into the shop. It was open to the street, with rows of low tables filling the floor, with only a few drunken men seated around them. Round paper lamps of green and gold hung from the ceiling, and the walls were painted garish pink and red.

Two of the rowdies from the front of the shop, took one look at Wei Fu, and pointed directly to the back.

Next to the kitchen was a large table. Fat Ang sat in the center, looking like a fat spider, spinning more webs. His dark blue robes were open at the collar and his cubby face gleamed with sweat. Beside him sat a laughing young woman. She wore her hair down, not in a proper bun, and the top two knots on her robe were undone. She giggled as Wei Fu came up, her head lolling.

"Master Wei!" Fat Ang said. He tried to get up, forgetting he was at a table, bumped into it, and fell back on his behind.

Everyone at the table laughed and laughed.

Wei Fu tried to do the same, to laugh as hard as they all did, while still swaying, supposedly not able to hold himself straight.

"You've come to celebrate," Fat Ang said, pushing the girl aside. She giggled again and fell to her side, then curled up like a kitten.

Wei Fu almost felt some stirrings for her, particularly when Fat Ang gave her such a possessive look.

But she, too, was probably beyond Wei Fu's means.

Instead, Wei Fu staggered over to the table and plopped down next to Fat Ang.

"Drink up!" he said, raising his own wine pot.

The table responded in kind, all raising glasses, then throwing the liquor down their throats.

Wei Fu managed to spill most of his, swallowing only the smallest mouthful.

Fat Ang looked at him, surprised. "I didn't know you, you, celebrated!" He laughed at his own brilliance.

"Celebrate. Yes." He looked back at the girl who was now softly snoring on the floor. "And mourn."

Fat Ang followed Wei Fu's glance with his own, nearly toppling over. "That's bad. That's really bad. You shouldn't be hurt like that. Have a new girl!" He snapped his fingers over his head and roared, "Tang! Tang! Another girl for my friend."

"But I want that one!" Wei Fu whined.

"No, no, take her back to my rooms," Fat Ang said, waving his hand toward the girl.

"I want *her*!" Wei Fu insisted, pushing at Fat Ang.

"She's mine!" Fat Ang said.

One of the other rowdies at the table said, "Shh. Shh. Here, have two girls. Not his."

"Who's the master here?" Wei Fu said, drawing himself up frostily. "You owe me. For everything."

"Sure, sure, you helped, you helped, but Mei Mei is mine, not yours," Fat Ang said.

"You weren't in my class," Wei Fu said, as if he was momentarily confused.

"Nope. Not smart enough for you." Fat Ang said solemnly. "But you told me everything. Everything I needed to know."

Wei Fu sighed, ashamed again that this false devil had taken him in so. He took an actual drink from his wine pot, swallowing some of the luke warm liquid that turned blazing hot in his mouth.

This idiot, this stupid peasant farmer, *had* used him.

And once Wei Fu got up the courage to attack him, to start a brawl, he could have him arrested and discredited. He might also be discredited, but he was willing to pay that price.

Wei Fu drew himself up, tugging at whatever bravery had ever lived in his heart. "Fat Ang, you are—"

"Fire!" came the hoarse cry from the street. "The law school! It's on fire!"

The nearby gate tower bells started ringing loudly. Everyone, drunk and sober alike, jumped to their feet.

Wei Fu abandoned the wine pot—no one could connect him with it, as his nephew had bought it. He didn't stagger at all as he rushed out the front of the shop with the others.

Mid-way across town, bright flames rose.

Even in the cool night, sweat instantly covered Wei Fu's back.

All of Da Shan was made of wood.

"To the buckets!" Wei Fu shouted, running down the street.

It was prescribed in the law that all of a town was responsible for a single fire. If it burned, everyone was charged with it.

Fortunately, other citizens had read the same law, and were already helping put out the fire by the time Wei Fu arrived, his lungs burning. The air was thick with smoke and it was difficult to see where to go, how to help.

As Wei Fu was turning toward the second line of men passing buckets along, he thought he heard someone calling his name, faintly.

Listening for a moment, Wei Fu heard a familiar cough. He turned and went back into the darkness.

Chao Xi was seated on the side of the road, his knees up, his head down. He coughed again, sounding hoarse and pitiful.

Wei Fu rushed to his friend's side. "What happened? Are you sick? Did you breathe in too much of the fire? Were you there?" He picked up his friend's hands. Even in the darkness of the street, he saw the cuts and burns on Chao Xi's palms.

"We must get you to an apothecary," Wei Fu scolded.

"No, no, I'll be fine." Chao Xi gave another racking cough. "Really."

"What happened?" Wei Fu said, getting his arm under his friend's and drawing him up.

"Home," Chao Xi insisted. "Take me home."

Grunting, Wei Fu turned. They walked slowly, Wei Fu taking most of Chao Xi's weight.

"It was only supposed to be the one room," Chao Xi murmured. "The fire—it got out of control so fast."

Wei Fu closed his eyes and stopped. "You didn't."

Chao Xi coughed again. "Most of the secretary's papers were saved. Along with the actual essays from the students."

"But not the recorded results," Wei Fu said, starting to walk again.

"They'll need to be re-recorded. By someone else," Chao Xi said firmly. "Seems the secretary also breathed in too much smoke, trying to save everything."

"I've been such a fool," Wei Fu said again. "Thank you, old friend."

"It was nothing," Chao Xi insisted. "Nothing."

"If you or your family ever needs anything. If that new son of yours needs a god-father—"

"Who else would I ask but an old friend?"

"Old friend, indeed."

Slowly, they stumbled through the street, a parody of drunken men, never exactly what they seemed.

The Dutiful Daughter

Mama Chen pretended not to hear Xi Bao's cries as she bent her adopted daughter's four little toes under while pushing her big toe toward her heel.

It wasn't that she didn't know how much the binding hurt—her own feet fit easily in the palm of one hand. But Mama Chen knew best.

"Please, don't do this to me," Xi Bao wept, the words echoing off the unpainted plaster walls in Mama Chen's windowless bedroom. She clenched her hands into fists, balling up the blue and silver patchwork quilt that covered Mama Chen's sleeping platform. At least she no longer tried to pull her foot out of Mama Chen's ancient hands: the beatings she'd received for such disobedience had finally made a difference.

"Shh, shh, Rare Treasure," Mama Chen said. "You're too big to be making such a fuss. Your cries even shame Chun Xing." She pointed with her chin toward the altar carved into the wall above the head of her sleeping platform.

Crimson silk embroidered with fine gold thread covered the bottom of the niche. Two dainty white porcelain cups filled with rice wine sat before a faded portrait of Chun Xing, the immortal. The outline around his bulbous head had been worn off by years of fingers seeking his blessing. Portions of his staff and the peaches he held were only visible through the eye of memory.

"I don't care!" Xi Bao wailed. "It hurts!"

Mama Chen slapped the girl across the face. "I expect you to be more brave," Mama Chen chided her. "You're getting too big for all this nonsense."

Xi Bao's black eyes flashed with a violet light, making her face appear as white as the snow on top of Tian Hiu and more ancient.

"Don't you look at me like that," Mama Chen snapped at her. "Who else would have taken in a bad luck girl like you? Wandering alone down Lichang street during Ghost month? When all the shops were closed and the owners gone? A girl who doesn't even remember her own name, let alone her family?"

Xi Bao took a gulping breath before she sighed and looked down. "I know, Mama Chen," she said quietly. "I'll try not to cry any more."

"Good girl," Mama Chen said, smoothing out the binding cloth as she continued to wrap the girl's foot, moving her skeletal fingers as quickly as she could. "We have to do everything we can or else you won't marry well."

"But I don't need to marry anyone here," Xi Bao said. "I will take care of you myself."

It was an old argument. Mama Chen didn't know who had originally raised the girl or why they'd told her she didn't need to marry. She'd often sworn silently at the stupid woodcutters, peasants, or whoever it had been who'd lost their child in the city, who hadn't realized what a beauty she was. Mama Chen had taken one look at her face and known that not a man alive would be able to resist her once she'd grown up. Even though a husband wasn't supposed to see the face of his bride before their wedding day, Mama Chen had worked out a plan how her Rare Treasure would be "discovered". Then they would move from the Xuanwu district and the noxious fumes from the kilns down the street.

"True ladies have husbands as well as tiny feet," Mama Chen told her. "And servants, who will do anything for their mistress. Even fetching her a thimble full of the Elixir of Life."

That was another of Mama Chen's deepest wishes, though she disdained from visiting the Taoists hidden on Meitau lane. They'd been chased away and their teachings forbidden by the Emperor, who'd claimed they were in alliance with the hoards of horsemen in the north. However, the philosophers and doctors had never actually left, just crawled between the floorboards and buildings like cockroaches. Mama Chen didn't trust their grave-stealing ways—the thought of medicine composed of powdered bones of her ancestors made her sick—but she was still jealous of their abilities and their long lives.

"Mama Chen, I'll take care of you. Always," Xi Bao promised.

"I know you will. And we'll live together in a large, prosperous household. You will be a good daughter to me." It wasn't that Fei Yu, Mama Chen's only surviving child, wasn't a good daughter, but Mama hadn't known that the charming Yi Shang was lazy, and a drunkard to boot when his parents had come to court them. Mama Chen's husband and sons had been killed in the battle of Tumu, when the dirty hoards had marched right into the city. She'd been desperate to find a proper mate for her sole child. His parents had been very clever, showing only the good side of their son. Now, he wasted his time and her daughter's bride money drinking and gambling, giving a mere pittance to the rest of the household, barely enough for them to live. He hadn't even the skill to get Little Fei pregnant, though he blamed it on their bad luck household, as well as the bad luck girl who Mama Chen had adopted soon after he'd arrived.

"Just me," Xi Bao promised. "I will take care of you myself. No one else."

"You will have many servants," Mama Chen said. She was ashamed of their small household. When she'd been a girl, her family had commanded handfuls of servants. Now, there was only Old Gardener who maintained the compound and his wife, Little Crane, who cooked for them. All of Mama Chen's brothers had married and had moved out to live with their wives. Since Yi Shang's arrival, they and their families only visited once or twice month.

As Mama Chen worked, Xi Bao cried out once more. However, the girl didn't ask her to stop. "Just me, Mama," the girl promised again, her wide eyes tinged with purple. "Just me."

囍 囍 囍

The winter that year was hard, and food, scarce. Mama Chen spent much time curled up under her quilts in her windowless bedroom—it was the warmest place in the entire compound. She dreamed of roast pork baked in the oven until its skin was crackling, and would wake, the imagined taste mingling with the salt of her tears. Her joints felt as though they'd been carved from unfinished wood and rubbed together roughly when she walked. She shivered under her blankets as the winter wind whispered in the eaves, and prayed to Chun Xing for a life long enough to see her family turn prosperous again.

Mama Chen tried to get Xi Bao to tell her about her former life, before she'd come to live with Mama Chen. The girl claimed not to remember anything, though one time she told of a dream: It was a somber place, cold and silent as a winter tomb. Two "men"—one with the head of an ox, and the other, a horse—carried a brave young soldier between them. He was very handsome, with a heart-shaped face and three moles that ran along the right side of his jaw.

"Oh!" Mama Chen proclaimed happily. "You dreamed of Jin Ren, my eldest son. Those two guards bring the dead to Yan Luo, the Judge of Hell."

"He was very handsome," the girl said quietly.

"He was. Maybe someday I will find him a bride." It was common for families to marry off their dead offspring, usually to form alliances. Mama Chen didn't have enough money for a bride price, but maybe someday she would—it would be an easy way to bring another girl into the household to look after Mama Chen when she was older.

Xi Bao grew sulky at Mama Chen's comments. She even started complaining about the cold until Mama Chen hit her with her cane and told her to go to her own room. Shaking and crying, Xi Bao left, cradling the arm that had been struck, glaring at Mama Chen with her purpled tinged eyes. Mama Chen wondered about the girl she'd brought into their house for the rest of the day, worried that she'd made a mistake, but forgot about her concerns during the night when a sweet voice came into her dreams told her that all was well, as it had many times before.

❀ ❀ ❀

Mama Chen lay on her sleeping platform at the dawn of the *Qingming* festival, sipping a restorative tea that Little Crane had made for her, every joint aching and telling her she was old. When Xi Bao came into her room, her spirits lifted. The girl walked with a curious gait, up on her toes like the dancer Lo Dan who'd escaped from the forest of swords by balancing on the tips of the blades.

"Mama Chen!" Xi Bao called happily. "See what I found for you!"

Xi Bao carried two stems of pussy willows in her hands, both male and female. The female branch was soft and silky, with beautiful, long, pale green blossoms and dark waxy leaves, while the male had brilliant yellow flowers, promising abundance. They would pin the stems to their robes to keep away any evil spirits who still floated nearby the graveyard when they went to clean their ancestor's tombs and pay their respects.

"They're beautiful," Mama Chen said. She didn't know where Xi Bao found the things she brought to Mama Chen, and not even beatings could drag it out of her. Mama Chen assumed that Xi Bao persuaded Old Gardener or Little Crane into doing her bidding, though she'd never gotten a straight answer from either of them when she'd asked.

Xi Bao helped Mama Chen dress in her finest silk outer robe, which was peach colored and had patterns of brilliant red bamboo embroidered on it. The cuffs on the sleeves had been replaced, and the shoulder seams had been resewn when the silk had frayed. However, Mama Chen could no longer afford to replace it.

Leaning heavily on her two canes, Mama Chen made her way to the Hall of Greeting, Xi Bao in her wake. Old Gardener had cleaned the hall from top to bottom at Mama Chen's direction the week before, knocking down the spiderwebs from the exposed roof beams, dusting the carved lattice windows, and polishing the fine black lacquer table. Red and gold painted tablets were artfully arranged on the wood altar at the front of the room. Each held the name of one of Mama Chen's ancestors. Sweet incense burned in a filigreed silver brazier set to one side, its scent mingling with the bright purple hyacinth flowers that lay on the other.

Fei Yu joined them there, and the three knelt on faded embroidered pillows to pay their respects.

"Where's Yi Shang?" Mama Chen asked.

"He's still sleeping," Fei Yu said, turning her face to hide her shame.

"Hmph," Mama Chen said, but she didn't send Old Gardener to wake him—the young ruffian was getting to be too much for the old man.

When they'd finished their prayers, they ate a lunch of cold cabbage soup and millet. Mama Chen recalled the feasts of her youth with ample portions for everyone, fresh fruit, and colorful ices, even this late in the spring. But she didn't complain too much that day—it was the *Qingming* festival after all—and it would have been disrespectful to her ancestors.

After lunch Mama Chen made her way to Yi Shang's room and rapped on his door with one of her canes. "Get up, you lazy dog! It's time for you to pay your respects to your family."

The door opened. Yi Shang wore an indoor robe, unbelted and crumpled, as if he'd been sleeping in it. Mama Chen wrinkled her nose at the musky, sour smell that came from his room.

"Go away, old woman," Yi Shang said, leaning heavily on the door frame. His eyes were bloodshot and his hair hung in greasy strands over his forehead.

"We're all going to the grave site together," Mama Chen told him sternly, raising one of her canes.

"It—a" The young man paused, his face growing pale.

"You'll be ready by the turn of the hour," Mama Chen said primly.

"I will," Yi Shang said, turning away.

Only then did Mama Chen notice that Xi Bao stood next to her. "See?" she told her adopted daughter as they made their way back to the Hall of Greeting. "Even a sluggard such as him can learn better manners."

Xi Bao didn't say anything.

Mama Chen wondered at the strange look of satisfaction her adopted daughter wore. "Smugness does not become a lady," she chided.

"I know," Xi Bao said, her features becoming more demure though her eyes still twinkled.

"Hmph," Mama Chen said, but she didn't scold her more.

Of course they had difficulty finding palanquins for Mama Chen and Fei Yu. Everyone in the city was visiting their ancestor's grave sites that day. Mama Chen groused about their loss of status since Yi Shang had come to live with them—if he hadn't been so useless, they would have been able to afford their own private chair.

"Shh, Mama," Fei Yu chided. "It isn't polite to say such things. Not out here," she added, looking at the crowded street.

"As a son, he should honor his ancestors," Mama Chen insisted stubbornly. "And what honor does he show me?"

"I'll take care of you," Xi Bao insisted. "I will always honor you."

"See? This is a proper daughter," Mama Chen boasted.

Fei Yu merely looked away and down. Mama Chen thought it was from shame, but then she caught a strange look of fear on her elder daughter's face. What could she possibly be afraid of?

Mama Chen turned her attention to Xi Bao. The girl looked beautiful, as colorful as a butterfly. Mama Chen had bartered one of her old robes for the outfit the girl now wore. The silk was as blue as an endless summer sky. "You remember what I told you? About Li Yan?"

"Mother," Fei Yu said, warning tingeing her tone.

"We need this alliance," Mama Chen said. "Li Yan's eldest grandchild would be a very good match for Xi Bao." It would probably be the best match he could make—he'd been born with one arm withered. Plus, Mama Chen and Li Yan had known each other since childhood: at one point, as very young girls, they'd even called each other sister. Mama Chen thought Li Yan would jump at the chance to align their families, to give them the opportunity to see each other more.

"But I don't need to get married," Xi Bao said.

Mama Chen held onto her temper and didn't strike the girl—beatings had never made her change her mind about this. "Why must you provoke me?" she asked instead. "You must make a good match to support you, to give you healthy sons."

Xi Bao scowled but at least she didn't reply. Why was she so set against marriage? It made no sense.

Finally Yi Shang and Old Gardener returned with two palanquins. "We will eat nothing but millet and cold soup for the next month," Yi Shang grumbled as the women got in. But Mama Chen couldn't complain. The palanquins were richly appointed, and the scent of sandalwood swirled around her as she stepped in. A fine cushion made of rich yellow silk covered the seat, and thin paper flecked with gold hung over the windows.

Xi Bao crept in next to Mama Chen and curled up by her feet. The main bridge out of the city to the burial grounds was crowded and their progress was slow. Fortunately, the day was sunny, and Mama

Chen passed the time telling Xi Bao tales of duty: of Koi An, the daughter who killed herself so her father's bell would ring sweetly for the Emperor; of Lan Te, who walked so many miles to bring fresh water to his old father every day that the gods blessed his house with a well right beside it; of the immortal Zhong Guo-Lao who tested the generosity of farmers and punished the ones who were stingy.

The cool air sent chills down Mama Chen's spine when she stepped from the palanquin. Laughter mingled with solemn chanting greeted her: many families were making an outing of their duty to their ancestors, and had brought colorful quilts to sit on as well as hampers full of roasted chicken, fresh spring greens and pickled fruit. Though the day was clear, pockets of haze blurred the air as families burned incense and paper money, honoring their dead.

Mama Chen let Xi Bao go ahead with Little Crane and Old Gardener, while she made her way slowly to their family plot, stopping and chatting with friends and her sisters-in-law along the way. She maintained a polite demeanor as they subtly boasted about their good fortune. Mama Chen praised their clever sons and bountiful daughters, certain that soon, luck would come her way again.

Old Gardener was helping Fei Yu rake the ground in front of the main grave when Mama Chen walked up. The leaves and dirt had already been washed from the beautiful green stone at the head of the plot, as well as the white "arms" that flowed on either side from it. Yi Shang, of course, was nowhere to be seen. Xi Bao was off to the side, cleaning the smaller grave of Jin Ren, Mama Chen's eldest son. Her heart swelled with pride at the devotion of her adopted child. The grave stone glowed in the bright spring sunlight, the dark gray shot through with purple lines.

"Such a dutiful daughter," Mama Chen told Xi Bao.

Xi Bao looked properly demure at the praise, her eyes downcast, her hand hiding her smile.

"Hurry up you two," Mama Chen told the others. "You've barely started and look at all the work Xi Bao has already done."

Fei Yu looked up. "It's not fair," she said, her jaw hard and stubborn. "Jin Ren's grave was already mostly clean."

"I cleaned it," Xi Bao declared.

Fei Yu glanced at the girl then looked away abruptly, as if she were afraid.

"You know you shouldn't lie," Mama Chen scolded.

"I'm not!" Xi Bao insisted. "I cleaned the grave earlier this morning, to show respect for my husband."

"What?" Mama Chen asked. "You cannot marry Jin Ren! I've adopted you." It wasn't proper for a sister and brother to marry, even siblings who weren't born of the same family.

"But I did," the girl insisted stubbornly. "I remember now."

"You remember?" Mama Chen asked. It was the first time Xi Bao had ever said those words.

However, before Xi Bao could reply, Yi Shang came up. He held a wine pot in one hand and a string of paper coins in the other. "They won't let me buy more wine with these," he slurred, walking onto the base of Mama Chen's father's grave, knocking sticks that had already been cleared away back onto it. "Guess we'll have to spend them here!" he giggled, a high pitched grating sound.

Mama Chen yelled at him. "Get off of there!" At Mama Chen's nod, Old Gardener hustled the drunken man away. Mama Chen put her hands together in prayer to hide how they shook with anger and humiliation as she begged forgiveness from her father.

Yi Shang shook off Old Gardener, then walked away before Mama Chen could say anything else. She sighed when she saw he was going to Li Yan's family plot, right next to theirs. Then Mama Chen had an idea. Maybe that fool could be of use. She called Xi Bao over to her. The girl still walked with such grace, even though her feet were smaller than budding bamboo. "Go and fetch Yi Shang. He shouldn't be disturbing Li Yan's family."

Xi Bao looked over at her brother-in-law. "I'll take care of him," she said softly.

Her words slid like cold winter rain down Mama Chen's spine, but she didn't think anything of it. She had her plan. "Make sure you're polite to Li Yan, and her grandson. Maybe he could be your husband someday."

"I already have a husband," Xi Bao said.

Mama Chen slapped the girl hard across her face. "Don't say that! It isn't right. He isn't for you."

The girl looked down and didn't reply, her fingers twisting together then apart, like twigs blown by a temple wind. Mama Chen knew she wouldn't get anywhere with the girl for now. "Go," she said. "Do as I've told you."

"I'll take care of him," Xi Bao promised again, then walked away with her strange gait, as halting as Mama Chen's own "lotus walk" but more balanced.

Mama Chen noted with satisfaction that Xi Bao was properly demure: she bowed so deeply to Li Yan Mama Chen was afraid she'd fall over, then she politely asked Yi Shang for help. When Li Yan stayed and talked with her, introducing her to her grandson, Mama Chen almost crooned with delight. Instead, she directed Old Gardener to start on the next grave.

On their way back, Xi Bao stopped and whispered something in Yi Shang's ear. Her eyes flashed purple and her face grew solemn and old. Yi Shang paled and was subdued for the rest of the afternoon, which made Mama Chen grateful.

It wasn't until they were leaving the graveyard that Mama Chen noticed that Yi Shang no longer wore his pussy willow stem. Fei Yu's was also missing. Mama Chen prayed fervently that night, hoping that the spirits hadn't noticed. She was visited in her dreams that night by the three-legged frog. Although he hopped away before she could take the gold coin from his mouth, she still believed it was a good sign.

At first, Mama Chen's dream appeared to be fortuitous. The luck she'd known was her birthright flowed in. Lin Yan came to visit and made discreet enquires about Xi Bao. Yi Shang spent more nights at the family compound. Though he stayed in his room instead of talking with them, at least he wasn't out gambling away what little money they had. Then Fei Yu announced she was pregnant. She had sickness every morning when she awoke and her belly began to round. Mama Chen spent much time on her knees, thanking every god she could think of. She bullied Yi Shang into giving them extra money so Little Crane could prepare special delicacies for the pregnant woman: fresh trout and water lily buds, goji berries soaked in tart wine.

However, as had happened too many times to count in Mama Chen's life, her good fortune began to slip through her fingers. Yi Shang grew pale and wan, whiter than swan feathers. Soon he no longer left his bed and within a month he died, wasting away, unable to eat or keep anything down. The smell of his room sickened Mama

Chen, as if he'd rotted from the inside out. They couldn't get rid of the stench, not even with specially blessed scented candles.

Fei Yu was devastated. Her morning sickness returned, worse than ever. Mama Chen's sisters-in-law came to sit with her, but nothing could console her, even their sharp comments about how she was making her baby sick with her mourning.

Only Xi Bao remained unaffected. She no longer cried when Mama Chen rebound her tiny feet, which were forming the most beautiful "lotus hook" that Mama Chen had ever seen, right in the middle where the toe and heel pressed toward one another. Xi Bao still walked more on her own than Mama Chen remembered anyone being able to do. She teased Xi Bao once about walking on lotus blossoms, which only made the girl give her a mysterious smile.

After visits from doctors they couldn't afford, secret potions smuggled in from the Taoists Old Gardener found, and herbs that Mama Chen's sisters-in-law pressed on them, Fei Yu still took to her bed months too early. The waters of life were filled with blood, and the baby wasn't properly formed. It had stumps along its torso, the buds of many arms. For all that it would have been a son, Mama Chen was grateful that it had never taken a breath.

Fei Yu never stopped bleeding after the birth and died the next day. Mama Chen felt the walls closing in on her. She knew it was impossible. Her room wasn't shrinking. It was just a trick her old eyes played on her. But there was no where else for her to go in her grief, and she couldn't go out in public during the first month of her mourning.

Then, on the fourth day of Ghost month, Mama Chen fell. She landed on her hip on the bare ground, but it felt as though she'd fallen on piercing daggers. Old Gardener had to pick her up and carry her to her bed. Mama Chen insisted that no doctors or Taoists be called—she would heal on her own, even though every movement caused her to pant in pain.

Xi Bao came to see her every morning, bringing her tea and thin soup for breakfast, then extra candles and lamps so Mama Chen could see to do her embroidery. She sat with Mama Chen, singing songs and telling stories. Mama Chen felt like screaming every day when she awoke, certain that her bed was shrinking along with the room. She said nothing though: she was determined to set a good example for the little girl, who strangely, became her only visitor. Everyone else was either busy or gone shopping when she asked about them.

After a week Mama Chen told Xi Bao to fetch Old Gardener—she wanted help rising from her bed.

"He's not here," Xi Bao said, tucking in the blue and silver patchwork quilt over Mama Chen's legs.

"Tell him to come see me when he returns from the market, then."

Xi Bao pursed her lips. "He isn't coming back."

"What do you mean?" Mama Chen asked, the chills racing down her spine having nothing to do with the walls of her room that were, in spite of summer's heat, still cool to the touch.

"After Fei Yu died, he and Little Crane talked about leaving. They said this house had too much bad luck. When you fell, I told them to go."

"But why?" Mama Chen asked.

"I told you. I would always take care of you. By myself," Xi Bao said proudly, picking up the tray that had held the breakfast things and daintily walking out on her toes.

Mama Chen shivered again. The walls of her room inched closer. Was there no one else here, no one else to help her? She tried to swing her legs to the ground, but even that much motion caused her to groan in agony. Needles spiked through the soles of her feet, and she quickly gave up trying to move. She'd heard stories of unwanted women locked up for decades, blind when they finally saw the sun again. Such a fate was not for her. She reined in her panic and tried to think her way out instead.

When Xi Bao came back in with her lunch, Mama Chen pretended not to notice the girl's smug smile. She said nothing but pleasant things throughout the meal, praising Xi Bao for her cooking skills. Afterward, she said, "You're taking such good care of me. You're such a good daughter. But I'm lonely. I miss the company of my sisters-in-law and my brothers. You need to send a message to them and tell them to come visit me."

Xi Bao looked thoughtful at that, however, she merely bade Mama Chen to have a peaceful sleep and that she would see her later that evening. Mama Chen was suspiciously tired after the child's suggestion. She purposefully curled her toes, hoping the pain would keep her awake, but her eyes closed in spite of all her effort.

When Mama Chen woke up, Xi Bao sat at the end of her sleeping platform, crooning softly to a tiny figurine she held in her hands.

"See!" Xi Bao said brightly when she noticed Mama Chen was awake. "There's no reason for you to feel lonely anymore. I've brought Fei Yu to visit!"

"You know you shouldn't—" Mama Chen's admonishment not to lie died on her lips. Xi Bao held a perfect replica of Fei Yu in her hands. The body looked as if it had been carved out of ivory, while the head was done in a different, more lifelike stone. Silky black hair was attached to the top of it, and cold eyes that stared at her had been painted on. Mama Chen swallowed down her sudden nausea. It couldn't be. Fei Yu was dead.

"Where did you get that?" Mama Chen asked, one shaking hand reaching for the doll. "Is this some evil Taoist thing?"

Xi Bao twisted away, not letting Mama Chen touch the doll. "She can't stay. I can't keep her away from the court for too long," she said, standing up and placing the doll next to the door, where it stared with unblinking eyes at Mama Chen. "Fei Yu said she missed you."

The doll didn't look sad, lonely, or like it missed anyone. It's face held an expression of sheer rage, as if it wanted to beat Mama Chen for her stupid, selfish plans.

"She also said she missed Yi Shang," Xi Bao continued. "But I'm not going to bring him back."

"Yi Shang is dead," Mama Chen told her, fear sending cold sweat down her back.

"And in the Third Burning Hell," Xi Bao said proudly. "I made sure. Now, don't worry about being lonely anymore, Mama Chen. I'm going to get you lots and lots of company. And servants too! Just like you always wanted." Her eyes turned purple again and her face aged.

"You're a good daughter," Mama Chen whispered, terror choking her voice.

"Daughter in law," Xi Bao replied. "I really did marry Jin Ren. He was so lonely in the Cold Moon Hell. He promised his soul to Yan Luo, to work for him forever in Hell, if I would take care of you as you have taken care of me."

Mama Chen blanched, remembering the girl's initial cries as she'd bound her feet, the beatings she'd been given. "I only did what I thought was best," she said, proud of how the stubbornness in her voice hid her fear.

"And now I will do the same," Xi Bao promised with a smile before she left again.

Mama Chen prayed fervently until Xi Bao returned, wishing she could curl up in a ball and float away, or that the hero Lei Zhen Zi would come with his golden sword and rescue her. She should have listened to the stories she always told, paid more attention to the lessons of wishing and pride.

In a short while Xi Bao brought in a small table—Mama Chen recognized it from Yi Shang's room. Then she left and came back carrying a large piece of ivory, half as tall as she was and shaped like a crescent moon. The outside curve was smooth and polished, and the lamplight made it look translucent. The inner curve had many figurines carved into it.

"This will be your court," Xi Bao said proudly. She ran her finger across the seat of an empty throne that had been carved halfway up the arch. "See all the people who will attend you?"

Mama Chen recognized many of the faces of the attendants, including Old Gardener, Little Crane, her brothers and their wives. Into a empty hole near the foot of the throne, Xi Bao now placed the figure of Fei Yu.

"I didn't know how I was going to fulfill my promise to my husband," Xi Bao confessed, her eyes completely purple now, the whites eaten away. Her hair was streaked with silver, and the lines in her face had sunk deep into her flesh, revealing her true demonic visage. "Not until you showed me how to fold my flesh." She held up one of her dainty feet. "Now, I know this might hurt, but you want to live forever, surrounded by your family, many servants, and great riches, don't you?"

Mama Chen shuddered as she felt the room shrinking, pushing her body against itself. "Why are you doing this to me?" she cried out in pain.

"Because I am a dutiful daughter," Xi Bao said. "And I promised to take care of you always." She began to sing a strange lilting song about the wonderful lessons of Hell, dancing across the ever decreasing floor, lotus flowers blossoming with every step.

Dragon's Son

"You want me to do what?"

Long Yen stood and drew himself up to his full height, staring down at the still seated, court-appointed white lawyer in his fancy gray suit.

The rocking hum of the air regulator sounded loud in the small space. Beyond the blond lawyer, who sat placidly with his hands folded on the scarred and rusted metal table, was the single door out of the windowless room.

It didn't matter if the door was locked, or if the lawyer and the guards had been careless. Long Yen couldn't take three steps down the hall before the emergency bells would ring, sending the miners scurrying out of the miles of corridors in the station and to their rooms. All the containment doors would slam shut, and when the authorities figured out which corridor Long Yen ran through, they'd lock him in, suck all the air out, and that would be that.

Even if Long Yen managed, somehow, to get outside, to the surface, it wouldn't be any better. Being a fugitive wasn't the problem: being topside was. It was possible to live there, just like it was possible to eat the recycling plant's sludge directly, before it had been given flavor and color and shape. He knew he was smart enough to be able to find a stronghold, join them sifting through the rough red dirt. But in that scenario, all he had was the slimmest chance that he'd find a trace of the precious minerals The Company hollowed out the planet for.

It was a life, but it wasn't really living.

"Yes, I can help you, Long Yen-san."

Long Yen narrowed his eyes at the lawyer. Given his flabbiness, he'd probably been born off planet. He'd obviously never worked the mines or corridors, not with his clean nails and unpocked face. Long Yen would bet that this lawyer had never been to the Chinese half of the station before, either. Where ever he was from, all Asians probably looked alike to him, and he hadn't bothered to learn that the planet of Da Chuan had been settled by Chinese a century ago, not Japanese.

"*Shur*," Long Yen instructed, folding his arms over his chest to hold his anger in, squeezing his calloused fingers against the scratchy prison jumpsuit. "*Yen-san* is Japanese. *Shur, Laoshur,* is Chinese."

The man's round blue eyes widened.

It would have been funny, and maybe Long Yen would have instructed him more, if he'd been at the Temple Bar, drinking with his cousins.

Here, it just made the load of rock between Long Yen and the surface feel heavier, the pumped in air a bit more stale. It reminded his aching heart that he'd never see his grandmother again, never know if the latest treatment had cured her.

"I apologize. Please forgive me, honorable *shur*." The lawyer pressed his hands together and bowed his head low—once, twice.

Long Yen sighed and didn't bother correcting the man's tone. "Whatever," he said, slumping back down into his chair again.

"Please, let me help you," the man said.

"Why should I believe you?" Long Yen said. He'd never heard of a court-appointed attorney even making an effort like this.

"Because I can get you out of here."

"By me telling you everything," Long Yen said flatly. "Everything about my family." *About the dragon's sons.*

The stranger leaned closer across the table, as if to speak a confidence.

Long Yen rolled his eyes. The hardened black ring embedded in the concrete ceiling in the corner heard every word, recorded every move. There was no privacy in an interrogation room. Even if Long Yen had a disrupter, there may have been duplicate, backup systems.

The man impatiently beckoned Long Yen closer.

With a sigh, Long Yen leaned forward as well.

"I found a loophole. Between the *qing lü* and the colony code."

Long Yen blinked, surprised. How did this stranger know about the ancient laws that the colony's code was based on?

For the first time, Long Yen felt a sliver of hope.

※ ※ ※

"You have such strong fingers, *xiao zi*, so clever, my little one," Nei Nei said, giving Long Yen a toothless grin over the tiny kitchen table.

Long Yen kept his smile to himself. He didn't want his grandmother's good mood to suddenly go sour. Not when she'd promised him a treat later, particularly if he'd been a good boy all evening.

The fan over Nei Nei's left shoulder made more noise than breeze in the sweltering kitchen. Dishes crowded the shelves on the walls, and the illegal ice box hummed only to itself in the corner, not connected to the station's systems.

Long Yen picked up another neon blue strand from the piles of glass-drawn wires strewn between them. The bright colors made them easy to see and weave, even in the dim light. He pushed back the hair dripping into his eyes, rubbing his fist across his sweating forehead, before he started to weave in the new strand, strengthening the net of electronic fibers.

The colors told him which way they ran. The red and blue were the weft, while the orange and black were the warp. He tried to be careful and not run his fingers along the wire: it would leave cuts all across his skin.

"*Xiao zi ma?*" Long Yen asked, pretending to concentrate, biting his lips together to keep from smiling as he teased his grandmother. "Just a boy?" Even though he had only turned seven, he felt much older and wiser than any of the boys who raced down the corridors just outside, who were Chinese, but not *family*.

"*Wo xiao zi,*" Nei Nei replied immediately. "My boy. My clever, clever boy."

Long Yen peeked up at Nei Nei suspiciously, but she still gave him a happy grin.

Maybe he was doing it right this time.

He pushed the strands together, drawing the weft along the warp, as Nei Nei had taught him. Soon, he tied off the ends and handed the net to his grandmother.

Nei Nei pulled on her work gloves and held the net up close to her face to examine the pattern. "*Hau, hau*, good," she said, nodding. "Now bring me my bag of plugs. Hurry!"

Sharp pins and needles pricked Long Yen's foot as soon as he put it on the scratched concrete floor. He'd been sitting too long on the hard metal kitchen stool. He shook his leg once, then stepped down on it hard, refusing to limp as he scurried across the room.

He knew better than to dawdle.

The bag of plugs was all the way on the other side of the room, next to the thin, fold-out futon that Nei Nei slept on. Normally, she kept the bag beside her at all times.

When the rough nylon straps pulled cruelly on Long Yen's fingers, he realized why. The wires he'd been working with had drawn unseen cuts across his flesh.

He'd forgotten a step in the process.

This was Nei Nei's way of teaching him to remember. She'd taught him early how to use the pain to help him focus.

The ache in Long Yen's foot receded while the fire in his hands grew.

Nei Nei still gave him her toothless grin, which looked innocent enough. He only now realized that her eyes were hard and merciless.

Still, Long Yen didn't drop the bag, or put it on the ground and tug it across the floor after him. He got it all the way to the table and even set it down lightly. Only then did he look at his hands and the ugly welts crisscrossing his palms, the chemicals of the bag reacting to the glass coating of the wires.

"What do I always say about wire work?" Nei Nei asked as she pawed through her bag.

"Sanitize everything," Long Yen said, turning toward the sink. Not just because of the cross-contamination, but to hide their not-always-legal work from The Company men.

He half expected Nei Nei to tell him it was too late, since he'd already been contaminated, he may as well just stay and help. But she didn't call him back. He found the grimy tube of sanitizing wash stashed under the sink, tucked in next to the antibiotic spray and black-market bandages. He carefully rationed out a small pearl of it into his reddened palm before he spread its soothing, cool gel over his burning hands.

Long Yen moved back to the table to watch Nei Nei wire the battery in. It was opaque, like the windows on the dawn side of the planet, as thin as the sheet Long Yen slept under, and as long as his thumb.

"Where do you think we'll catch the best signal?" Nei Nei asked as she worked.

"Council room kitchen hallway," Long Yen said. His heart beat harder in his chest as the silence between them spun out, only disturbed by the sound of the rocking fan in the small kitchen.

"Bold," Nei Nei finally replied.

Long Yen had tried to calculate the risks and rewards, as Nei Nei had taught him. He was pleased that she approved of his idea.

"Ceiling?" she asked as she pinched the ends of the battery and drew it longer, making it fit better along the side of the net.

"Behind the recycling pipe. The outgoing channel." People threw things they shouldn't into the recycle chutes all the time. No one would think it strange that a tiny electronic current showed up there.

"Clever monkey."

Long Yen bit his lips together and didn't reply, didn't let himself react.

The *bizi*, the white boys he'd met on one of his daring explorations of the other half of the station, had called him a monkey. But he was no *honzi*.

True, a monkey could climb the wall to get to the pipe, but only a *tian she* could worm its way behind the pipe, snake along the passage unseen.

Only a true dragon's son could tap into the communications network for the entire station with a simple woven net and not get caught.

※ ※ ※

Long Yen listened to the white lawyer (Ken? John?) recite code and verse of the *qing lü* as well as Nei Nei or any of the other hall lawyers. He kept his eyes narrowed and his lips pressed firmly against each other, not showing the slightest bit of emotion. He'd worked hard to eliminate all his tells, precisely for a time like this.

"So you see," the lawyer (Tom?) ended with. "Section 3.14, paragraph 7, implies that the supplicant can be freed."

Long Yen spread his hands out across the tough metal table. It was too warm in the room for it to be cool, but old habits of always seeking the coldest spot died hard.

"'Freed' could be interpreted any number of ways," Long Yen said slowly, considering. "Like freed from the prison of life, if they took a Buddhist approach." That's what Nei Nei had always said, and what she'd asked for if she kept getting sicker, if the treatments didn't work.

"That's where the *Xi* code comes in," the lawyer said eagerly. "It's been applied against the *qing lü* before, for exactly such an interpretation."

"It won't work," Long Yen said, considering the possibilities. "No, the council lawyers will tell you that you've been tricked by the *bi sai*, the shell game. The family—" he paused, realizing that he'd just admitted that there was a group, something beyond just him. "*My* family, has too many pieces in play. The council lawyers must have something else, information you don't know about. They'll twist any confession I make to something else."

The lawyer shook his head and gave Long Yen a crooked smile. "Pieces in play. Like a shell game. And how do you win the shell game? By never hiding the *zhen zhu* under the cup in the first place."

Long Yen sat back in his chair so he wouldn't correct the man's pronunciation, but also to mask his surprise.

Why had this court-appointed lawyer, with his fresh white face free of the pockmarks of malnutrition, mention the *zhen zhu*, the pearl? Did he know something more than he could say, particularly under the merciless recording eye of the council? Had he actually been placed here by the family?

Hiding the pearl, as one might in a shell game, was a long con. Longer than the one Long Yen had been running.

Hope ran cold fingers, colder than the night side of the planet, down Long Yen's back, raising chicken flesh across his shoulders.

"Tell me more," he demanded, leaning forward, aware that he was catching at the stranger's net, as if it might save him.

❇ ❇ ❇

Long Yen slouched in the outer corridor with the two other money changers. They were recent immigrants to Da Chuan—Russians—trying to carve a niche out for themselves. The family tolerated them in their half of the station for reasons only known to them. Long Yen thought they belonged in the other half, with everyone who wasn't Chinese. Let them make a living there.

They stood close enough to the airlocks that the filters couldn't completely clean the air of dust, so a thin red haze filled the enclosed space, muting the sharp lines of boxes and pipes that ran along the ceiling and up and down the curved tunnel walls.

The sound of the blowers was louder here. The sifters from the surface, who sometimes came inside for trade, liked it that way. They called the sound the blowers made *niao ge*, canary song: If it ever died, they knew to flee.

Long Yen had been practicing his lifts all month. Nei Nei had nearly scalded his fingers with boiling water when she'd seen how sloppy he'd gotten. She'd made him start with family first, his cousin, that stupid ox, Xin Chao. They'd practiced in the tiny kitchen, bumping shoulders, slipping hands in and out of pockets, grabbing IDs and cash.

Once Long Yen had fingers like a snake again, Nei Nei sent him back out to the corridors, first practicing on miners at shift end, when they were slow and not perceptive. Long Yen had to steel himself to stand and watch, his heart pounding. Not because he was afraid of being caught, no. But because watching them made him realize that without the family, he might have turned into a living ghost like them.

Then she sent him after council kids, who Long Yen could have been in school with, preparing for the final exams. He gladly took their trinkets and toys, keeping one of the fancier chronometers for himself, that showed planetary time plus the long count of when the next supply ship would arrive. The station was self-sufficient, and had been from the start, but the planet couldn't support a large enough population to justify factories to create luxury goods.

Finally, Nei Nei declared Long Yen ready. He only knew his target by the red and white scarf she wore to hold back her hair. All the miners wore the same dull gray jumpsuit, which Xin Chao swore were modeled after prison clothes. The only way to tell one from the other sometimes was by the way they decorated their nametags.

Long Yen worked with the money changes for a week, not even looking for his target until two days before, when he'd seen her heading for the mines. Her shift would end now, and Long Yen planned to get close enough to her. Once his job was finished, he'd still have to work as a changer for another week.

It was part of the family's constant teachings. Never make any sudden appearances or disappearances: The goal was to blend and flow, and not be remembered.

As the workers started shuffling out of the mine, Long Yen pushed himself up with a suffering sigh, hiding his true excitement. He held his hand out, first finger extended, then started making circular motions with his hand, indicating his trade: changing The Company script for hard cash that was good anywhere in the station, not just The Company store.

First the men came out, row upon row of sleep walkers, swelling the corridor with their ranks. Long Yen never met the eyes of any of them, never tried to see if a man's soul still remained. He knew they couldn't steal his own life from him like a hungry ghost, but the fear remained. The only sound was the blowers and their soft footsteps through the red dust. None of the men talked or laughed.

Long Yen knew the women were coming because at least a few of them still gossiped together. He thought he spotted his mark as he concluded his business with the last man, her bright red and white bandana bobbing in a sea of yellow, purple, orange, and pink.

Why was she special? Why did Nei Nei insist on her ID? And why here and now?

Long Yen marked her progress, cursing his luck. She was mid-tide in the sea of miners. How could he reach her?

It looked as though he'd be stuck here for two more weeks.

Suddenly, the money changer in front of Long Yen shouted and shoved the miner he was doing business with away, shouting, "Thief! He steals my money!"

The man fell straight against the girl.

It couldn't be luck. It had to be family.

Didn't Nei Nei trust Long Yen to do the job?

The supposed thief flailed his arms, as if trying to regain his balance.

A bright red line appeared on the cheek of the girl. He'd cut the girl with a hidden knife.

Long Yen hurried to her assistance. "Let go!" he yelled, pulling the girl free, rushing her along, plucking her ID easily from her pocket.

"I'm fine, I'm fine, thank you," the girl insisted.

Long Yen nodded and let her go, turning away before she got a good look at him.

She tugged him back around before he could make his escape. "You're not hurt?" she asked.

Long Yen glanced at her face, then away again, quickly. "No, no, I'm fine," he assured her.

He couldn't afford to see her wide brown eyes, or her face as round as a portal window.

"I need to help my friend," he said, bowing and keeping his head turned away. "Excuse me."

Long Yen melted into the crowd as quickly as he could, sliding into the next corridor before the police arrived, the white mice with their nasty biting teeth, dragging him into the council rooms.

He passed the ID over to Nei Nei without looking at it, not questioning, not this time.

He still couldn't help but see the miner again, when her face was plastered all over the screens at the Temple Bar. She was being presented as one of the brightest of the new batch of students who'd passed the civic exams and were moving into government positions.

Or at least someone clean, and well-fed, who happened to look exactly like the miner, who also bore a striking resemblance to one of Long Yen's older cousins.

The worker's card and blood must have been clean, and a close enough match, so the cousin could pass, and the family could gain a new stronghold.

Long Yen raised his glass in a silent toast, though he would have unseen her if he could.

Too much knowledge, particularly for a dragon's son, was never a good thing.

※ ※ ※

The lawyer still sat. His recording stick, a dull white bar about the size of an antique Mah Johng tile, sat in front of him on the table.

Long Yen paced around the tiny interrogation room as he talked. He knew it didn't matter: the stick picked up every gesture, every nuance, as well as his heart beat, flush rate, and other tells Long Yen couldn't control or train against.

The air regulator still hummed in the background, totally inadequate to draw out the heat and humidity two men generated. Even the dark red clay walls were beginning to sweat.

"So you had access to all government communications," the lawyer said (Chris, maybe?) "And you had an agent in the council."

"Civil service," Long Yen corrected.

"Would you recognize her again?"

Long Yen shrugged. "Maybe. Maybe not. Depends on how important she is. If it was important enough to keep her hidden, she'd have a new face by now. Subtle changes—shifts up or down her cheek bones, flattening or sharpening her nose." She wouldn't have a moon face anymore.

"All right. Anything—"

A loud bang exploded just outside the room, ending with a sharp sizzling sound.

Long Yen froze. The family wouldn't rescue him. He wasn't important enough. They might kill him, but not like this, not big and flashy.

Maybe something had gone wrong in one of the tunnels?

Xin Chao, Long Yen's cousin, threw the door open. Before the lawyer could rise from his chair, Xin Chao shot him with a sizzler, the black net spreading over his chest, burning into his face.

Long Yen grabbed the recording stick from the table and snapped it in two.

There was an official recording, of course. But the family also had access. They must. How else could they have found what room he'd been hidden in?

"Come on!" Xin Chao said, sticking his head back out the door, his sizzler at the ready.

"Where are we going?" Long Yen asked, following close behind though he wanted to keep his distance. Xin Chao wore all black, like some crazy ninja from the screens. Just a brief glance had told Long Yen too much: how small Xin Chao's pupils were, how little he sweated, how unsteady he was on his feet.

It was no safer with this great ox than on his own.

Only two guards lay in the hall. Long Yen felt something between pleased and insulted—on the one hand, only two men had been scoured, but had he only rated two guards? He'd have thought there would have been more.

"Nei Nei's gotten worse," was all Xin Chao said.

That hurried Long Yen along. "Then the last treatments—"

He stopped at Xin Chao's headshake.

"So don't you upset her," Xin Chao said sternly, pulling Long Yen up close, breathing hot, stinking breath in his face.

"I won't," Long Yen said easily. He would have promised the crazy man anything.

"You'll do what she says?"

"Of course," Long Yen assured him.

He didn't know what price Nei Nei expected for his rescue, but he knew it would be high.

He was willing to pay it.

Xin Chao grunted and shoved Long Yen into a tiny utility closet. Thin plastic shelves ran along one rough dirt wall, covered with rusted pipes. Dials and readouts blinked steadily on the other.

Nei Nei crouched like an overgrown basket of rags at the far end. Clear tubes hooked into her nose and fed her air laced with illegal opiates. Thin wires ran from the iron collar around her neck, snaking up to her temples and down under her white cotton blouse. They kept the seizures to a minimum, though she still twitched every few minutes.

But her brown eyes were still dark and clear, and she grasped Long Yen's hand firmly with hers.

"*Xiao zi*," she whispered. "My boy."

Long Yen crouched beside her. "What do you want me to do?"

The muffled sounds of containment doors clanging shut sounded around them.

"There's so much you don't know. So much left to teach you."

Nei Nei twitched hard, then she brought her other hand up to his cheek.

He kissed her overly warm palm. "You have time to teach me," he told her, keeping his voice steady, his tears locked away.

"There's only one thing to tell you," she said with a sad smile.

The closet walls shook. Dirt scrabbled loose and trickled down to the floor.

Fear gripped Long Yen's heart harder than Nei Nei's firm hand.

"*You* were the pearl, my son."

"What? I don't understand—"

"Now, promise me," she said, holding his wrist tight enough that he wondered if there would be bruises. "In *cunwang*, you always choose life. Not death. You hear me? You must choose life for yourself. Live beyond all of us. You were always hidden away. Like the pearl. You must come out of the clouds now."

She jerked his hand toward herself suddenly, slapping it against her flabby belly.

The hard press of the haft of a blade scoured Long Yen's palm.

He jumped away, pressing his back against the rough wall.

Nei Nei slumped in her chair, her blood blossoming across her stomach like the fire of a supply ship at takeoff.

"What have you done?" Xin Chao said as he came rushing in. He bent over, looking more closely at Nei Nei's wound.

A winking light in the corridor caught Long Yen's attention, but he didn't turn toward it.

He couldn't, not yet. Not until he'd done his duty. What he'd promised to Nei Nei.

Reaching his long arms out, Long Yen snagged a pipe from the other wall, and brought it down hard on Xin Chao's unprotected head.

Long Yen then held up his hands and dropped to his knees as the soldier approached, the targeting light on his gun winking still.

A taped confession of the family's doing would never have been enough for the loophole the lawyer had found between the *qing lü* and the colony code.

Not enough to show true contrition for his crimes.

Only by decisively turning against the family could that loophole be exploited.

Only now could Long Yen beg for forgiveness from The Company, and be truly freed.

※ ※ ※

Long Yen stood and stretched up, his face a moon blossom, always facing the portal that showed the stars.

Up and up they went, this strange new crew buzzing around him. Since it was his first time out of orbit, they let him wander from one port hole to the next, drinking in the sweet cold nectar of the night.

As gravity loosened its hold and Long Yen began to float, he tethered himself to the hole, the stars blazing like tiny pearls.

The cool metal edges of the ship's walls trembled under his hands as the thrusters engaged and the ship turned.

For the first and last time, Long Yen saw Da Chuan. It hung like a frozen red marble in the sky, shrinking away until it, too, was just a dot of light.

One of many, all loosely connected by the string of humanity.

Finally, Long Yen turned away, turned toward the enormity of his task, the one Nei Nei had set for him.

It had been easy to accept his banishment, to know he'd never return to Da Chuan. The family had been prepared for this, and had a secret receiver ready to be implanted just underneath the new dragon tattoo that itched on his bicep.

The pearl had never been in the game, at least, not the little local game.

No, the family had always wanted a bigger game, with more shells, more cash.

More planets.

And as a true dragon's son, what could Long Yen do but blend and flow, move out and beyond, free to fly among the clouds at last.

The Tortoise and the Maiden

Bing Yu gratefully placed her buckets and the yoke she'd used to carry them beside the ancient stone well that served the town of Ie Gou. The day had dawned hot, she'd forgotten her hat, and even carrying the empty buckets had left her dripping.

Not that it mattered. Bing Yu brought her hands before her, looking at them with shame. Her skin was no longer lotus white, and her fingers had grown stiff with hauling buckets and serving platters, losing their cleverness with needle and thread.

With a sigh, Bing Yu looked at the well, dreading the hard work ahead of hauling buckets full of water up to fill her own. She knew she must hurry: Though Mother had seemed better that morning, the wasting disease that had left her mother in such pain and unable to walk generally grew more fierce as the day progressed. And Father was still away, trying to replace the fireworks he'd been swindled out of, and wouldn't return for two more days.

But instead of starting, Bing Yu looked out and away. Drowning fields of rice stretched out in all directions from the collection of dust-covered, one-story clay buildings that made up Ie Gou. Though Bing Yu's family was made up of merchants, they still prayed like farmers: to Taiyang Shen for sunshine, and to Ying Long for rain, each in the right amount, in the right season, so the rice would grow and the town, prosper.

Just beyond the flat fields rose outlines of mountains, hazed with mist and heat. Bing Yu couldn't tell how many *li* away they stood, or even which peak grew before another. So many poets had tried to describe their grace, but Bing Yu liked "misty mountain crowns" the best.

Oh, to fly to those far peaks! Bing Yu took a deep breath, already smelling the fresh air sure to swirl around the tops. She closed her eyes for a moment, imagining the calm and beauty of the tall pines, how their sweet fragrance would seep into her skin, the soft call of the birds attesting to the beauty of the place, the quiet and peace.

Then Bing Yu shook herself. She opened her eyes, glancing around, ashamed. What was she doing, staring off at mountains she'd never visit? Wishing for things she'd never have? She wasn't like her foolish father, paying good *cash* for mere dreams, leaving their family disgraced, no one shopping at their store, surviving on crumbs from her mother's family, her aunt smiling cruelly all the time now.

Bing Yu returned to her task. The wheel lowering the bucket into the well squealed loudly, and the wood groaned.

The splash of the bucket in water startled Bing Yu. It was much sooner than usual. She hoped that was a good sign, that maybe her luck, and that of her family's, was changing.

Bing Yu strained as she pulled the heavy bucket back up. At one time, she wouldn't have been able to lift it. Her shoulders had also grown more broad, stronger, just as her hands had roughened.

No one of good standing would want her as a wife anymore.

Bing Yu sloshed water on chest as she drew the bucket over the edge of the well, gasping as the cold struck her skin. She looked down in dismay: the entire front of her shirt was wet. It was indecent.

At least no one was there to see.

Then Bing Yu realized a brown oval bumped around in the bottom of the bucket.

Her luck was as bad as it had ever been. The water was ruined. She'd have to draw more. Hopefully the well itself wasn't infested, or the water tainted.

With sure hands, Bing Yu braved the cold water and reached for the shape.

It veered away from her suddenly.

Startled, Bing Yu nearly pulled her hands out of the water. Then she pushed them in further, grabbing the thing, hauling it out of the water and dropping it next to the well.

An ancient head snaked out of the oval, then its legs.

It was a tortoise.

A very special tortoise. Esoteric symbols had been painted in silver on its vaulted, yellow-and-brown shell. Its eyes stared up like black pearls. Hard scales, like red pebbles, covered its arms, while a sharp beak grew down over its mouth.

Bing Yu wondered briefly about tortoise soup: Maybe that would help heal her mother?

Then the tortoise spoke in deep, grating tones. "Thank you, Miss. I was trapped down there by unscrupulous traders."

Bing Yu hid her surprise by bowing low. Her grandmother, and her mother, had told her tales of magical arrows and talking animals, but she'd never believed them. "It was nothing, auspicious sir," she assured him. "Anyone would have done as such."

The tortoise chuckled. "Ah, but most would have then threatened to cook me, or else dropped me back into the well."

Bing Yu's cheeks flushed, but she didn't tell him she'd been thinking just that. She stared at the tortoise for a moment, while he stared right back.

Then Bing Yu shook herself. She needed to get back to the family compound. "Excuse me, good sir, but I must finish my chores," Bing Yu said with another bow.

She looked at the bucket full of well water. Was it clean? Should she dump it by the side of the well? Or was it actually blessed, since it had been in contact with a magical creature?

The tortoise gave a hooting laugh.

Bing Yu's cheeks grew hotter and she bit her tongue so she wouldn't say anything rude. She'd been raised better, no matter their current circumstances. She wasn't like her aunt.

"Get yourself fresh water," the tortoise instructed. "Pour what you have against the wall of the well, so I might have a drink."

Still blushing, Bing Yu did as the tortoise directed before she lowered the well bucket again.

The unblinking stare of the creature sent chills against Bing Yu's damp skin. Though he wasn't a man, she would have sworn he leered watching her work in her wet shirt.

"You're new to this," the tortoise exclaimed after Bing Yu had filled her first bucket and was lowering the well bucket again.

"I am," Bing Yu confirmed.

It wasn't her place to say anything else, how her foolish father had been swindled, promising the local council a grand fireworks show for the spring festival, only to have not a single stick light or even spark. How Old Cook and Gardener had run away, and no one would serve her family, so all the work had fallen to Bing Yu's now broad shoulders. How people stopped shopping at their general store, walking instead to the far side of town to the shops there.

How hard it was to be treated like she was nothing, after being taken care of and respected her entire life.

The ancient tortoise nodded, as if listening in on Bing Yu's thoughts.

"You must let me help," he said gravely. "In payment for freeing me."

Bing Yu didn't reply as she hauled up the full bucket. She wanted help. Her family needed it. But it didn't feel right accepting help from such an odd being. Besides, what could he do?

"Is it your mother who is sick? Or your father?"

"How did you know?"

"You smell like *li shr*," he explained.

Bing Yu nodded. It was true. The medicinal herbs the old Taoist had given them had stunk up the entire compound, and hadn't done a thing.

Finally, Bing Yu replied, "My mother," as she hauled the bucket over the lip of the well, this time not spilling any as she poured the water into her own bucket.

"In the Emperor's city, great *stelae* have been raised, surrounding the central market, covered with cures for common ailments."

"You've been to the Emperor's city?" Bing Yu asked, envious.

"There and beyond," the tortoise assured her. "Tell me what ails your mother. Maybe I can help."

The tortoise seemed so sincere. Despite her misgivings, Bing Yu told him about the pain in her mother's legs, how she could no longer walk, how it now seemed to eat away at what was left of her.

The tortoise appeared to be listening, though he wove his head from side to side like a snake. Then he stopped, and merely stared.

Bing Yu wanted to cover herself with a shawl.

Finally, the tortoise spoke. "Have you tried making a tea of hare's ear?"

"Rabbit ears?" Bing Yu asked, dismayed. They didn't have money to buy fresh rabbits.

"Don't look so dismayed. It grows wild near the water fields. The leaves are pointed, and the flowers are yellow, blooming in a large spray, like fireworks."

"I know that flower!" Bing Yu exclaimed. She'd seen it before and had thought it very pretty. She hadn't realized it might have medicinal powers.

"Use the roots, and mix them with peony flowers."

"Thank you," Bing Yu said, bowing low. She wasn't sure it would help, but she also didn't think it would hurt. She hefted her yoke over her shoulders, careful not to spill any more water.

"I must go now," Bing Yu said, giving the tortoise one last shortened bow (the yoke really was heavy) before she turned away.

"When it works, will you give me a kiss?"

Bing Yu's cheeks flamed at just the thought of it.

"I will not!" she called over her shoulder as she hurried away.

Her father may be foolish, paying far too many string of *cash* for ruined fireworks, but he hadn't raised a fool for a daughter.

※ ※ ※

The cure worked.

After just a few days, Bing Yu's mother started feeling better. She welcomed the return of Bing Yu's father still from her bed, but at least she was sitting up, with the window open and the lamps lit, fresh summer breezes playing with the edge of her bright green quilt.

At the end of seven days, Bing Yu's mother took her first tentative steps from her bed and out into the garden at the back of the family compound. Fat peonies, colorful tiger lilies, sweet jasmine, and happy pansies still bloomed, though weeds were starting to infest the ground beneath them, and the dead leaves hadn't been trimmed away. No one had time to care for the flowers anymore, now that the gardener had run away.

The family had gathered on the small brick deck, dressed in fine robes and laughing over the children—Bing Yu's brother and his cousins—playing a game of charades.

Joy filled Bing Yu at the sight of her mother sitting with their family. She wasn't fully well, but if the gods answered Bing Yu's prayers, it was only a matter of time.

If only she could say the same thing about her father, and their disgrace. Though the council was willing to let him provide the fireworks for the end of summer festival, he hadn't been able to find any at a decent price. He'd lost so much *cash* already, and other merchants cheated him regularly.

When her aunt caught Bing Yu's eye, she leapt to her feet like the servant she was becoming, rushing off to the little alcove where the cooking stones still roasted in the morning fire, ready to heat water. An inadequate roof covered the cooking area, that didn't guard against the afternoon sun, and was small enough that when it rained, the water dripped directly onto the back of anyone standing there. Plus, the fire pit was so low it made Bing Yu's back hurt when she bent over it too long.

No wonder Old Cook had run away the first chance she'd gotten.

Bing Yu vowed that when her family grew rich again, she would make her father spend his money more sensibly, in particular, a bigger cooking alcove with proper shade.

In the Emperor's city, Bing Yu had heard that tea was made from special leaves, grown on the mountain side, harvested by special collectors by hand, then dried and twisted. She made "peasant's tea" instead, out of the flowers from the garden; dried chrysanthemums, bright pansies, and soothing nettle.

While Bing Yu waited for the pot to steep, it didn't surprise her to hear the grating tones of the old tortoise from behind her.

"You don't belong her," he admonished.

The strange markings on his shell gleamed brightly, as if painted with moonlight. His eyes still shone midnight black and he stared at Bing Yu as if he could see through her blouse, making her blush. Behind the sharp horn of his nose, his mouth looked downturned, disappointed.

"I am where I need to be," Bing Yu replied honestly enough. She was no servant girl, her family were merchants, not cooks. But she also needed to keep the peace between all the members of her family, especially her mother and her aunt.

The tortoise scoffed. "Not just here. No. This town."

Bing Yu's heart leaped, as if it would jump straight to the peak of the misty mountains, dragging her with.

"My family is here," Bing Yu replied quietly. It was unthinkable for her to just go off on her own, no matter how much her caged heart hurt to stay.

"I could take you with me, when I go," the tortoise said softly.

One thing Bing Yu had learned early: Everything had a cost. "At what price?"

"Let me spend the night with you, in your bed."

Bing Yu laughed, lighter now. "Payment up front, then," she asked as she poured the tea into her aunt's highly-prized tri-colored cups. "I don't think so."

"But you could disappear after we got away," the tortoise whined.

"And so could you, after that night, never fulfilling your promises."

"I wouldn't—"

Bing Yu cut the tortoise's protests off. "My honor is worth more than that. Plus, who would look after my family if I left?" No matter how much she might long for mountains she'd never climb, her family came first.

"Ahh. What if I looked after your family, first?"

"Could you provide fireworks?" Bing Yu asked. She knew she was bargaining with something priceless, the once-in-a-lifetime gift of her virtue, for an evening of flashy colors that would disappear in the mist.

"That's what frequently happens when the jade plays with the pearl," the tortoise leered.

Bing Yu's cheeks flared hotter than the cooking fire. "That's inappropriate!" she exclaimed. How dare he make such jokes with her?

"Miss, I didn't mean anything by it. Yes, I can provide your father with fireworks. It will be the most spectacular show this valley has ever seen."

Bing Yu knew he lied—he had meant something by his earlier remark. He was as immoral as all tortoises.

But he would also live up to his promise.

The tortoise disappeared. Bing Yu picked up her tray and strode back to the garden.

Somehow, she was going to trick the tortoise into giving her everything she wanted, while she kept her maidenhood intact.

※ ※ ※

The tortoise had lived up to his word. Her father couldn't believe the price he'd gotten for a whole cart full of fireworks. He'd tried out a few to make sure they were good, also to prove to the council that he would fulfill his word this time, and not bring more bad luck to the town.

Bing Yu worked to keep her promise to herself as well. Though her father was at the store almost all the time in the days before the festival, protecting the fireworks from any harm, she still snuck into the back without him knowing, stealing four old sacks that had held rice, as well as the remains of an old, silk robe.

One of the things Bing Yu had learned about hare's ear: While the roots had made good medicine, the long, floppy leaves were spicy enough to burn her lips when she carelessly brushed her hand against them after stripping the plant.

This had given her an idea.

Using straw and reeds, Bing Yu fashioned a body out of the sacks, then had covered it in silk. She hoped that in the dark of her room, the tortoise wouldn't be able to see the difference. Her fingers still remembered how to use a needle and thread, though her new calluses caught on the fine cloth.

Bing Yu took extra care with the private parts of her stand in, blushing the entire time. She filled the whole crotch area with hare's ear leaves, while leaving mere suggestions of mounds for her tiny breasts.

Though the fake body was heavy, Bing Yu easily lifted it onto her bed the night of the festival, grateful for once for her strong shoulders.

That night, Bing Yu and her family sat in a prominent place in the town square, close to the council. While her father was proud of the honor being paid him, Bing Yu's aunt said it was just so they'd be able to grab him quickly when the fireworks fizzled again.

"Hush," Mother said sternly.

Bing Yu felt as though her world had just righted itself again. Her mother and her aunt fought all the time, but since her mother's illness, her aunt had pushed, and her mother had given.

Maybe things could get better again.

Everyone in the square gasped as the first beautiful night flowers lit up the sky. Sparkling lights of green, red, silver, and gold exploded above them. Children clapped their hands and shrieked, while the old men proclaimed it the best display they'd ever seen, that even the god Zhu Rong would be envious of such a show.

Happier than she'd be even in the mountains, Bing Yu walked beside her mother after the show, her ears still ringing with the loud explosions, her face sore from holding back an inappropriate grin as the council congratulated her father. Mother had agreed to interview a new cook, and Father had promised Bing Yu more time in the shop, where she could watch over him and prevent any more foolishness.

Just before they got to the happy red gate of their family compound, Bing Yu saw a round stone looming.

"What was that?" Mother asked as it quickly scuttled away, out of the light of their lanterns.

"Nothing," Bing Yu said, though her happiness had evaporated as quickly as the bright colors of the fireworks.

The tortoise had come to collect his prize.

Bing Yu fondly bid her parents goodnight, blessing them and thanking the gods for their good fortune, making her way quickly to her little room in the back. She blew out all the lamps, hung cloth over the window, and lay down *under* her platform bed, shivering against the cold dirt.

"There you are," she heard the tortoise from above.

Good. He'd appeared on the bed, as she'd hoped he would.

"Your skin is so soft!" he exclaimed.

Bing Yu heard a rustle of silk. She wondered if he was rubbing his head against the cloth. She felt a little sick to her stomach, but she pretended she was enjoying it.

"That feels good," she whispered.

"I can't wait to see you."

"You can't, good sir," Bing Yu told him. "My aunt would see any light shining from here, and come to see if there was a problem."

"I understand." The tortoise chuckled. "You're very clever."

"No, I'm not. This is my first time," Bing Yu confessed. She didn't need to fake the trembling of her voice. "I'm not sure what to do."

"You just lay there and I'll do all the work," the tortoise promised. "First, a trip down to your beautiful jade gate."

Bing Yu blushed at the thought of what the tortoise was doing, where he was going. She'd made an indentation for him, like a heavenly channel.

She heard him slither around, then he paused. "Is something wrong?" she asked, afraid he'd noticed her ruse.

"That's it! You smell like hare's ear. You continue to make the tea for your mother?"

"Of course," Bing Yu told him.

She heard him grunt a little, and she cried out, like she knew a good bride would. "That's not enough," she gasped.

"What do you mean?" the tortoise growled.

"I'm ashamed to say," Bing Yu demurred.

"You must tell me what you need, how the hen should grow her teeth."

Bing Yu hadn't heard that expression before, but she guessed. "I like—I like a little pain," she whispered. "When I pleasure myself. You should bite me."

"Oh my dear, I knew you were the one for me," the tortoise said, his gravely voice growing deeper. "Are you sure?"

"Use your teeth," Bing Yu instructed.

The tearing sounds above her made her shudder.

She couldn't help her smile at the sudden howl.

"My mouth! My mouth is on fire! Oh, you are too much for me!" the tortoise exclaimed.

With a flash, he was gone. The hare's ear had worked.

Bing Yu spent the rest of her days alone and unmarried, and she rose to great prominence in both the town and her family, known as the matriarch who always gave the soundest council as well as had the most clever plans when bandits and tax collectors came their way.

Sisters

Lin Han still knelt in the courtyard, as still as the towering rock *stelae* behind her that the names of her family's ancestors were carved into. The bleak early morning light washed everything gray: the hard brick she knelt on, the black iron brazier in front of her, the twisted pine in front of the double wall that stood guard before the door leaving the family courtyard. The sacred smoke from the brazier had long since disappeared, but the heavy smell of burnt wood and paint still hung in the air.

Double-hour bells rang in the distance, muffled by Lin Han's fog. She felt herself stirring, as if she were waking, though she hadn't slept all night. She blinked dry eyes and stiffness poured through her body, as if she were suddenly no longer young. Her knees started to ache. Her shoulders felt weighed down, as if a yoke with buckets filled with water lay across them, like the laborers she saw in the street. She took a deep breath, the taste of smoke mingling with the tears still gathered at the back of her throat.

Lin Han curled her fingers into fists on her thighs, realizing how cold the tops of her hands were when they touched the warm silk. She pushed herself forward, trying to rise, and ended up catching herself with her hands, the cold hard brick pushing back at her. Her legs were filled with sand, leaden, hard to move.

Slowly Lin Han rose. She swayed like young bamboo in a storm trying to gain her feet.

As if that was a signal, Old Cook scurried out.

"Please, Miss, you must go to bed now," he whispered urgently.

"No. I will not leave my sister," Lin Han said.

Old Cook didn't have to say it. She heard it echoing again against the hard bricks of the courtyard, the proclamation by her mother, her father.

You no longer have a sister.

"Enough of that," Lin Han said, banishing those ghosts of memory. "I must take her with me." Sometime in the night a plan had come to her.

Old Cook opened his mouth, then closed it and gestured at the huge brazier. It had *Fu* dog heads on the sides, each bigger than Lin Han's head. Ornate legs curved down to splayed toes. It had taken six men to haul it into the courtyard.

Lin Han had grown the last year, and so it merely came up to her chest now. However, she would never grow big enough to carry it away.

"Fine," she said. "I need, I need..."

The chill of the morning finally entered her bones. She shivered abruptly and swayed again. But she refused to give in to the horror of it, what she needed to do.

"I need something to hold her in."

"Right away, Miss." Old Cook bowed low before racing away.

The long shadows of the courtyard wall to Lin Han's right began defining as the sun rose. The twisted pine took on long needles and distinct branches. The brilliant red tile on the rooftops beyond the courtyard sprang to life. All around the quiet courtyard the city of Yen Tu woke up. Already the street venders with their buckets of millet porridge and clear chicken broth called out their wares. People walked in the street, snatches of conversation floating up over the wall.

Lin Han just waited.

Old Cook came back out with an ornate, porcelain, red-and-white vase. It was skinny at the bottom and blossomed out at the top. Hard nubs of white stuck out from the body in curling lines.

Dao Ming would have wanted to put tall lilies in it, something graceful and overflowing.

Lin Han accepted the weight of the vase, cradling it in her arms for a moment before taking the cold metal scoop that Old Cook also handed her. She stood on her toes and looked into the brazier.

The pile of ash was so small, like Dao Ming had been.

Mama would kill Lin Han for handling ashes. She'd insist on a cleansing ceremony from the stinky Taoist priest with the dark robes who never smiled as well as a second one from the Buddhist priest in his bright orange robes who was more sour still.

Tears gathered behind Lin Han's eyes again. This was all she had left of her younger sister. A burnt spirit tablet, taken from their ancestors' altar in the front greeting room.

A hard spike of hurt pierced her chest as she remembered how her parents were going to deny Dao Ming's birth, just like they'd denied her death. They claimed now that there had only ever been two children: Lin Han and her older brother. Dao Ming had been written out of the family records. Father had talked of bribing the census takers to cross out her name. All her clothes had been given away or burned. Her favorite straw-stuff doll destroyed.

Last night, Mama and Father hadn't even held a funeral, barely said a single prayer before they'd placed Dao Ming's spirit tablet in the brazier.

Someone had to do something for Dao Ming. There was nothing to anchor her spirit. She would become a red-faced angry ghost, stealing food and paper ghost money meant for others.

Lin Han's tears fell as she stuck the shovel in the ashes. The mound crumbled, the fine ash sliding away like sand. When she lifted the first scoop, the early morning breeze puffed away some of the soot, sending it dancing across the courtyard.

She carefully tipped the scoop into the vase so no more of the ash escaped. Moving slowly, she completed her task, though some of it had spilled onto her fine dark-blue robes. Mama would be mad, but Lin Han didn't care.

Finally, Lin Han stepped back. With a bow, she solemnly handed the small scoop to Old Cook, who just as solemnly took it.

"I will bury this," Old Cook assured her.

Lin Han swallowed around a dry mouth. "Thank you," she whispered, touched that he was treating Dao Ming's burnt spirit tablet like a body, as if they were actually handling the dead.

"You take care of Little Miss," Old Cook instructed. "We will hide you as well as we can today, me and the gardener and your mother's dressing maid."

"Thank you," Lin Han said again, bowing low.

Though her family might deny Dao Ming, Lin Han was still going to see that at least in the afterlife, her sister would be taken care of.

※ ※ ※

Lin Han stood on one side of the dusty street, looking at the Taoist priest's shop on the other. The tiny wooden shack sat nestled between two larger stone buildings, almost as if he'd blocked off an alley to make his home. No paint decorated the walls, no mystic symbols were carved into the wood. Just a hand painted sign, weathered gray wood with bright red paint promising suitable mates for all.

The mid-morning bells had already rung. A few laborers remained in the street, squatting under the eaves of one of the stone buildings, rolling dice and drinking strong pear wine. They hadn't seemed to notice her—no one had. Lin Han knew her fine blue robes didn't belong in this part of Yen Tu, knew that the vase she carried was worth more than a few *cash*.

Either Dao Ming protected her, or Lin Han had also turned into a ghost.

Finally, the old man she'd watched go into the Taoist's shop came out. He clutched a brown leather bag tightly to his chest as he hurried off. Maybe the old Taoist was also an apothecary, though he didn't have a sign for that.

Feeling great daring, Lin Han stepped out of the shadows and into the brightly lit street. She rushed across though there was no traffic, no people or palanquins to avoid this far from the city center. She fumbled with the latch and had to use her elbow to push on it so she wouldn't have to put down the vase.

The dark of the shop made Lin Han stop and blink her eyes for a moment. Spicy medicine smells, the scent of burnt *jing* sticks and incense all came to her, as well as long boiled tea and sweet chrysanthemum. The Taoist sat silent and still behind the counter against the far wall. Rough wooden floorboards snagged her sandals as she walked forward.

Jars bigger than her vase filled with bulbous white roots in yellow liquid hung from ropes from the ceiling. A long dried snake skin marked with a black diamond pattern stretched from one of the room to the other and swayed in the slightest breeze. Eggs cooked in tea sat in another jar on the counter. The back wall held row after row of sealed porcelain jars, all meticulously labeled with either red or black characters.

The Taoist rose from his seat. His long face ended with a hanging jowl and his forehead lifted up to a bald skull. Fringes of greasy white hair curled down from just above his ears, over his shoulders. His nose hung like a foreigner's and his ears stood out like long handles.

"Good day," he said, giving her a small bow. He voice belied his skeletal stature, ringing from him like a deep bell.

"Good day," Lin Han said. She hugged the vase closer to her, the hard nubs pressing into her chest. "I need to find a mate."

At his raised eyebrow, she made her voice stronger. "For my sister."

She carefully lifted the vase out to show him, missing its hard pressure against her chest. "The ashes...the ashes of her spirit tablet are in here."

"Ah, a *minghu*," the Taoist priest said, nodding. "A spirit wedding."

"You must find someone who will look after her. She was, she was a good girl. She will work hard. But she should also be respected. Honored."

"Thank you for honoring me with your request," the Taoist said gravely, giving Lin Han another bow.

Relief made Lin Han sag where she stood. She'd done the right thing gathering up the ashes.

"Tell me," the Taoist said over steepled fingers, looking down at her from his tall height. "How old was your sister?"

"She was eight. Her name was Dao Ming."

The Taoist came around his counter and stood in front of Lin Han. He bowed very low to her, then knelt down so he was closer in height to her. "I'm so sorry," he said. "But Dao Ming was born in the year of the Ox."

"She was," Lin Han said.

The lump was back in her throat.

"I cannot find a mate for her," the priest said simply.

Surprise took away some of the sting.

A grown up, speaking so plainly?

"Why not?" Lin Han said.

"She's too young. She can't even have a funeral. Veneration is only right from the young to the old. The other way, from someone older to someone so young—it isn't the natural order of things. And brides, as you know, are very honored."

"Please," Lin Han whispered. The room had suddenly grown very dark, and the medicine smells clogged the back of her throat.

"I'm sorry. But I can't help."

The Taoist reached across and turned her gently toward the door.

Lin Han felt as light as a leaf blown by the wind, no weight to push back.

Before she could think she found herself outside in the bright sunshine.

A group of boisterous students were walking by in the street, causing Lin Han to shrink back under the eaves. She stood blinking, her breath heaving.

Of course the adults couldn't help. They hadn't been able to help after the accident, when Dao Ming had been hurt.

A wailing sound startled Lin Han. She pressed her back against the rough wood of the Taoist's shop. Where was it coming from? The sound of clashing cymbals and drums rolled out next, meant to scare away any bad spirits.

From down the street she saw a group of men carrying something on sticks over their shoulders, a palanquin she assumed. Someone very important. As they drew closer, she saw she'd been wrong.

They carried a paper-wrapped wooden coffin.

On top of the coffin was a painting of the dead: a young man with stiff black hair, a sharp nose, and kind eyes.

Lin Han carefully watched the funeral procession, picking out his mother and father, his younger brothers, and the other relatives.

No wife.

As if sleep walking, Lin Han found herself drawn out of the shadows, following the procession.

She would find a mate for Dao Ming, one way or another.

❀ ❀ ❀

White grave stone embraced the hill outside of Yen Tu. Lin Han followed at the tail of funeral, still clutching her vase. Her head felt light, like a feather fluttering across the road, while sand chained her body to the earth, heavy and slow with exhaustion.

Wailing mourners shrieked at the front of the procession, followed by the musicians banging cymbals and drums to chase away any evil spirits attracted to the dead body.

The graves nearest the entrance hadn't been cleaned in several months—probably since the last *qingming* festival that spring: leaves littered the curving white stone and bright grass marred the smooth lines.

Lin Han vowed to come out and clean her sister's memorial place every month, not to wait for the annual tomb sweeping celebration.

As Lin Han followed the procession up the hill her heart lightened. Only those with a proper rank were buried up on top of the hill. This meant the family not only had money, but power and placement.

It wouldn't matter if the family found another bride for their dead son: Lin Han would make sure he married Dao Ming first. Any other brides would be second or third wives. Not first.

The clanging cymbals and drums started to get louder, the pace, faster. Lin Han hurried, catching up to the stragglers in the procession, then pushing her way forward. No one stopped her. She didn't wear the proper white mourning clothes over her robe, but her face was still streaked with ashes and tears, so she must belong.

A Buddhist priest in bright orange robes stood at the head of the grave. He was a tall, pompous man, the kind who smiled at children but then treated them as if they couldn't understand even the simplest words.

Lin Han knew she wouldn't get any help from him.

The parents of the boy stood beside the priest. The mother wept loudly while her husband and sons consoled her. Lin Han looked at them closely.

Would they be kind to her sister?

They were kind with each other. Maybe they would welcome Dao Ming, too, if their son visited one of them in a dream and told them about his wife.

The paper-wrapped coffin sat poised over the grave, balanced on the long poles used to carry it from the town. Alongside each pole was strung a strong rope.

When the priest finished his prayers and blessings, the laborers came forward. They slid the poles away while holding onto the ropes.

Lin Han stood poised, right beside the grave, the ashes of her sister's spirit tablet still clenched tightly to her chest.

As was custom, everyone in the funeral procession turned their back as the coffin started to disappear into the earth.

Lin Han didn't care if the laborers saw her: they wouldn't say anything, not to the family. It wasn't their place.

So she tipped the vase and scattered the ashes on top of the coffin.

Dao Ming and her intended would be buried together. Their funerals would be held together, because now all the prayers said for him would be for her as well.

It was as good an introduction between the families as any.

囍 囍 囍

Lin Han waited for the priest to finish the funeral under the fragrant pine trees in the graveyard. The family was still wailing, and they were burning incense. She'd learned her sister's future-husband's name—Tu Shr. The empty vase sat beside her. She was so tired. She just wanted to sleep. But Dao Ming must be married, first.

The early afternoon breezes tugged at Lin Han's hair. She gathered twigs to her, stripped the bark down and used it to tie the sticks together, making little figures. The one with the sprig of long soft needles from a yew tree was Dao Ming. It didn't really look like a skirt but it was the best Lin Han could do. Tu Shr's had a knotty twig across the top, like big strong shoulders.

Lin Han hid behind the tree as the procession started back down the hill. She didn't want anyone to ask her any questions. There she found the cap of an acorn that she also gathered up.

As soon as the last person had reached the bottom of the hill, Lin Han raced back up. The laborers wouldn't fill in the grave until later, closer to twilight, when light ran away from the world. In three days time, the younger son would return and take a cup of the dirt back to the family that they would use to represent their dead son on their ancestors' altar, replacing the spirit tablet which was buried with the body.

At the edge of the grave, Lin Han found three trampled pieces of paper ghost money that hadn't been thrown into the grave, money the dead could spend in the afterlife. She wished she had more, but she couldn't climb into the grave and ever hope to get back out.

The three pieces would have to do for the bride price, what the groom's family gave the bride's.

Lin Hand made a small pile of dirt on the left side of the grave and placed the figure of Dao Ming there. She formally presented the bride price to her, wishing she had a red envelope for the money. She tucked the money in under the little figure. On the right side, she created a second pile, and placed the figure of Tu Shr there.

When everything was set, Lin Han picked up Tu Shr. Carrying him well above her head to honor him, she did a couple of dancing steps as she walked around the top of the grave to the other side.

"Look Dao Ming! The wedding procession has arrived!"

Lin Han kept Dao Ming in one hand while she hid Tu Shr in the other. It wasn't proper for the couple to see each other yet. Then she danced back to the other side.

"Dao Ming! You've arrived at your husband's house now. It's so big!"

From the top of the hill, it almost seemed that way. Tu Shr didn't control all of the graveyard and ghosts from his high point, but she could pretend.

Finally, Lin Han brought the two stick figures together on the mound of dirt. She didn't know the words the priests would say, so she sang a hymn to Xi Wang Hu, asking her for blessings on the couple: May they never grow hungry, may they have many children, and may they always be honored.

Lin Han placed the acorn cap next to Dao Ming, telling her, "Drink up! Drink your wedding cup!"

Then she placed it next to Tu Shr, telling him, "This is your bridal cup. Drink and be together forever."

Lin Han stepped back, bowed her head and closed her eyes to give the happy couple a moment of privacy.

Exhaustion slammed down on her and she swayed. The wind played with her hair, stronger now. Maybe a storm was blowing up.

When she opened her eyes, Tu Shr had slid down on the dirt mound so his head was now close to Dao Ming's.

Lin Han clapped her hands. Tu Shr had surely accepted Dao Ming as a bride! Her sister had a husband, someone who would look after her and treat her with respect.

Lin Han bowed low to the happy couple.

Normally, what followed would be the wedding feast. But there wasn't anyone else to celebrate.

"I will eat for both of you later," Lin Han promised as she picked up the figures, holding them together in the palms of her hands.

"The goddess will look out for you and bless you always," she promised as she opened her hands over the edge of the grave and let the figures tumble onto the paper coffin below.

They landed on a bit of clean paper, not where every member of the family had dropped a handful of dirt.

Lin Han gave them the acorn cup, and the ghost money as well.

She didn't know what to do with the vase. It didn't belong in the grave. She couldn't take it home: it was just one more thing of her sister's that her family would deny.

Instead, she planted it firmly at the head of the grave. Maybe when the younger son came back to get the dirt for the ancestors' altar, he'd see the vase and use it instead. That way, both Dao Ming and Tu Shr would be venerated.

After one last low bow, Lin Han turned away from the grave and started down the hill. She was too tired to skip or dance, though she knew she should—she was still part of a wedding procession.

But her feet dragged on the earth and her tears started again. No one else would ever know what she'd done, how she'd taken care of her sister.

Still. She'd finally managed to find her peace.

About the Author

Leah Cutter currently lives in Seattle--the land of coffee and fog. However, she's also lived all over the world and held the requisite odd writer jobs, such as working on an archeology dig in England, teaching English in Taiwan, and bartending in Thailand.

She writes fantasy set in exotic times and locations such as Tang dynasty China, WWII Budapest, rural Louisiana, and the Oregon coast.

Her short fiction includes literary, fantasy, mystery, science fiction, and horror, and has been published in magazines as well as anthologies and on the web.

Read more stories by Leah Cutter at www.KnottedRoadPress.com. Follow her blog at www.LeahCutter.com

About Knotted Road Press

Knotted Road Press fiction specializes in dynamic writing set in mysterious, exotic locations.

Knotted Road Press non-fiction publishes autobiographies, cookbooks, and how-to books with unique voices.

Knotted Road Press creates DRM-free ebooks as well as high-quality print books for readers around the world.

With authors in a variety of genres including literary, mystery, fantasy, and science fiction, Knotted Road Press has something for everyone.

Knotted Road Press
www.KnottedRoadPress.com

www.ingramcontent.com/pod-product-compliance
Lightning Source LLC
LaVergne TN
LVHW011735060526
838200LV00051B/3175